A Haunt of Jackals

A Haunt of Jackals

I.O. Adler

Lucas Ross Publishing

Contents

A Haunt of Jackals
by
I.O. Adler
Old Chrome Book Three

Published by Lucas Ross Publishing.

Edited by Dave Pasquantonio, www.davepasquantonio.com

Author website: ioadler.com

Chapter One

Shadows wended their way across the lot between plastic-wrapped pallets of construction material. The long arms of a building printer lay partially assembled near the gate leading to the road. A half-moon brooded behind the high clouds and cast an insufficient glow through the skeletal beams of steel standing on the concrete slabs.

Dark figures scurried past the raised foundation towards the site's generator and an excavator hunched on its tracks.

Too dark to see faces.

But Miles Kim had three targets.

His Insight module painted a red square center mass on all of them, losing one momentarily when the line of sight became interrupted. But the intruders stuck close enough together, no longer running, moving casually now as if out for a late stroll instead of trespassing on a secure building site in the middle of the night.

Maybe that's who they were. Drunks on the way home from nearby Jumbo's Trunk bar, kids taking a shortcut, or vagrants too lazy to make the Church of the Sands shelter for anyone in need of a cot.

Miles popped on his flashlight. The brilliant white beam caught the trio in its broad cone. Three men dressed in dark clothes, one carrying a bolt cutter and a duffel bag, the other two with jerry cans of sloshing liquid.

"This is where you turn around and leave," he said.

The three only hesitated for a moment before spreading out.

Miles kept the beam moving between them. Mentally assigned each target square a number. "Fence and the gate you cut through are back behind you."

"Get that light out of my face," Number One said.

Number Two flashed Miles with a headlamp. "Go back to your trailer, old timer."

Three spoke with a stutter. "He's a m-metal head!"

Miles sighed. "Last chance. This is private property. Turn around now, or the militia gets summoned."

Number One had the bolt cutters. "Maybe we clip the scrap off him and throw him into the recycler."

Two set his jerry can down. "No, perro. Some of that junk's worth a lot of credits intact if you know how to cut."

"W-we should go," Three said.

Number One took a step forward, the bolt cutter swinging. "Thought you were good with maths. He's an old man, and the creaky bot isn't even armed."

Miles flexed his metal right hand. "What this creaky old bot does have is an Amber Drive Series arm- and-hand mod. You heard of Amber Drive? Big back in the day when Meridian wanted its repaired soldiers to have something for close quarter combat. Nothing as fancy as slicers or finger blades. But who needs those when you can snap a neck or crush a windpipe? You punch an opponent just right, you can tear out their guts. Made 'em illegal after the war. The fancy refined mods you see these days don't hold a candle to the Amber Drives. You know the worst part? Sometimes when you grip something, the hand squeezes and can't be made to let go, even after the operator's death."

He wriggled his fingers. The three trespassers stared, their mouths open.

"Correction," his Insight module piped up inside his head, polite-as-you-please. *"Your arm is a Stoner Bionics 14, your shoulder is generic Meridian open-source design, and your hand is model—"*

"Shut up, Insight," he murmured.

He eyed all three men before setting his flashlight onto the dirt and straightening up. He flexed his neck and rolled his head and ignored the soft pops from his back.

"L-let's get out of here," Three said.

Number Two led the way, and the three were running by the time they made the gate where a portion of the fence had been cut and peeled aside. Once there, they had trouble making it through the gap as Three became caught by a wire. He had to drop his jerry cans and lost his sweatshirt. As his companions pulled him to the opposite side, they ran off into the night.

Miles watched them leave. A dog was on the nearby sidewalk and barking, first at the three intruders, then at Miles.

He examined the fence. Something for the report. He crossed the yard to retrieve his flashlight and to collect the dropped cans. The reek of gasoline lingered. A quick survey, and he could see no damage had been done to anything on the site.

A snuffling came from behind him. The dog had snuck in through the fence and was standing behind him. Its amber eyes glowed.

"Shoo! Go home!"

The dappled hound ducked as if it were about to bolt. But it held its ground.

He stomped his foot.

The animal shied back. Followed him when he headed for the trailer. The white shoebox structure served as the foreperson and architect's headquarters by day and the guard shack by night.

Tristan sat inside, leaning back on a swivel chair, his security outfit's shirt unbuttoned and sleeves rolled up, showing both tattoo-covered arms. His feet were propped on the desk. Miles had saved him a few weeks before, a near-drowning in a greenhouse fishpond. He had also served as Miles' driver, had informed on Miles to a corrupt cop, and had agreed to Miles' offer of a security job when the boss requested an additional warm body. A complex relationship.

A wall screen had a local news report, but the volume was muted. Something about an explosion or impact in River City, which was being blamed on the Caretakers.

A headline blinked. *Kinetic Strike Kills Two Hundred*.

Real or fake news? Hard to know. He lived in Seraph now. River City and her Meridian Corporation overlords were the past.

Another monitor displayed a hazy image of the front gate and the far corner of the property. Neither had caught the three trespassers cutting their way in. Miles would have missed them if he hadn't been on his way to relieve himself after one too many cups of tea.

The dog whined from outside the door.

Miles examined his cup. The remaining tea had grown cold. He dumped it and filled it with water from the sink before setting it outside. The dog eyed the offering warily before slinking forward and lapping it up.

Tristan yawned and flashed his yellow teeth. "Did I miss anything?"

"Just the local wildlife. Anything new on the incident?"

"Not at this hour. They're just looping the earlier report. I guess they're still up there, aren't they?"

"The Caretakers? Who knows? It's all speculation for now."

Tristan scratched absentmindedly. "Why can't they just leave us alone and we leave them alone? Starting up the violence again, and for what? Or maybe...maybe they're going after Meridian and River City, and they'll leave Seraph out of it."

"Last time I checked, the Caretakers weren't fond of anyone."

"Yeah. Yeah, you're right. I'm tired. Four more hours and we go home."

Miles turned off the news. "Watching the time doesn't make it go faster."

"It lets me know how much more sleep I can get. Because once I go home, Yasmin hands off the twins."

"Maybe you should have thought of that before accepting this job."

"I thought it would be quieter. You slamming the door, the tea kettle, your device vibrating, and now that whining. Is that a dog out there?"

Miles ignored the question as he grabbed for the device he had left on one of the other desks. Two missed calls from Marshal Barma. He hadn't heard from him for weeks since the matter with the Fishes had been laid to rest. Why was he calling at this hour?

Barma picked up on the first ring. "Kim, where are you?"

"The security guard gig Santabutra set me up with. What's up?"

"I've got a situation and I wanted your input."

"Can it wait until the end of my shift?"

"No. There's been a shooting and I have no idea where to start with this. I'm sending you the location. Get here quick."

Chapter Two

Miles drove Tristan's three-wheeler through the dark streets past the cargo containers, which made up the bulk of the shanty town on the west side of Seraph. Insight labeled the neighborhood Bright Blocks, as if the cheery name could obscure the fact that a good portion of the district's residents lived in squalor. The weak headlights barely illuminated the uneven road.

He navigated down the ever-narrowing lanes until crossing a flood protection berm. The cargo containers gave way to the Seraph dump, a sprawling landfill with several scrapyards operated amid a trash-strewn stretch of wasteland. While fences marked several properties, most of the wide space was nothing more than competing heaps of refuse. Hulks of abandoned vehicles lined the side of the road. Drums with unknown contents lay partially buried. Dark stretches of dirt glistened as brown liquids congealed on the ground.

Even the most desperate among Seraph's residents avoided living here. Warning signs hung askew on posts and the remnants of rusty galvanized steel barriers—*Keep Out. Danger. Hazardous Material.*

An acrid stench stung Miles' nose. Tristan's wagon had no side windows or doors.

Miles slowed to a crawl and checked his device. Took a turn past a tall mountain of broken furniture and printed goods. Stacks of cargo crates large enough to house small vehicles lined the way. The ground grew muddy. Miles didn't dare drive any faster lest the vehicle get bogged down.

The location Marshal Barma had pinged was close. What could possibly be out here? The rational question yielded to the facts of Miles' own experience as a cop. Bad things happened in remote locations.

A subcompact electric vehicle stood parked by a collection of massive containers. The containers stood open and dark. Miles parked a few paces away and left the headlights shining as he killed the engine and got out.

Barma's imposing form appeared at the threshold of the largest steel box. "Turn off those lights."

Miles did.

The marshal switched on a flashlight to illuminate the ground. "Took your time coming."

"Early morning traffic. Please don't tell me you called me here to remind me I don't know my way around town."

"Don't you have a computer in that robot head? This way. And mind your step. The floor gets sticky."

The cargo container's interior was damp and stuffy. Cardboard and carpet remnants lay stacked on the floor, congealed and rotting. Their feet squished as they walked to the back of the container. A dangling curtain marked a doorway cut in the steel. A faint glow emanated from the space on the other side.

Barma shoved the curtain back and stepped through. "Watch the edges. It's sharp."

A second container lay on the opposite side. Bare metal floors and no rust. A single bulb dangled from a wire in the center of the space. A table sat beneath it. And sprawled around the table next to knocked-over chairs lay three bodies.

Miles let out a sharp exhale. "You brought me here for this?"

"Call it what you will. I want a second opinion. And don't put your foot in anything important."

"I know the drill."

Miles crouched and surveyed the scene. Three firearms lay scattered nearby, two burners and a sawed-off shotgun so short it might as well be a pistol. One burner was chrome, a model with four to six shots, personal defense, and not much use otherwise. The second burner was something law enforcement might carry, capable of augmentation uplink, a twelve-shot battery, high power for a laser pistol. But the battery light was winking red. The shooter had emptied it.

All the weapons were close enough to have been dropped by the three victims. There were personal devices on the floor as well, along with blood from one of the fallen.

"Checked for vitals?" Miles asked. "I assume you did, since there's no ambulance here."

"They're all gone."

Miles shifted closer and shined his own flashlight. All three men were well dressed, relatively neat, groomed, and clean, at least until the event which marked their demise.

The first body, the closest, was a middle-aged white male, patterned silk charcoal suit, a wide necktie with mauve and silver horizontal stripes, and a matching pocket square. Buffed fingernails and cleanly shaven. He had been struck by the shotgun in the chest.

The second man lay on his side, his face partially concealed. Brown skin, older, thin, balding, with long white sideburns. His slender, almost skeletal fingers still touched the chrome pocket burner. He wore rings on his hands, gold, and most were studded with gems. Tidy laser holes marked his left arm, throat, and cheek.

Miles had to maneuver to examine the third man. The largest of the three, he had fallen backward with his arms out. His yellow coat lay open, revealing his ample stomach and a bright starched white shirt marked with a tiny burner wound over his heart. His sun-bleached blond hair was thin and gelled and looked like a raised palm fixed to the back of his head. A pair of AR glasses sat askew on his face, but Miles didn't see any visible augmentations that would link with the device.

"All wounds are front-facing," Miles said. "Appears that they shot each other."

"Yup. And?"

"Everyone was seated and getting along well enough. None of them look like they live anywhere near here. The one with the glasses might have been recording what went down. I'd check all their devices. Doubt they were meeting for a card game in this dump. Something shady, no doubt."

The marshal grunted. "No doubt. That's all police 101. I didn't call you out here for that."

"All right. I'll bite. Who are they?"

"You really haven't been around here long." Barma used his light to illuminate the big guy in the yellow coat. "Bing Patton. He's the owner of the Yellow Tigers militia, or at least the closest thing. He's the largest stakeholder and president of their board of directors."

The thin man was next. "Shahid Khar. If you know the Seraph underworld, you know him. He has fingers in every pot. Information broker. He knows where all the closets are and put some skeletons in there himself. He has leverage on so many people, he could move Seraph a hundred klicks in any direction, if he decided it would make him a profit."

Finally, Barma directed the flashlight to the man in the silk suit. "And that's Xander Trowbridge. Old money. Knew the elder Fishes when Seraph was little more than a big camp next to the old springs. Water baron, owns more land than anyone should, whether illegally or by rule of law. Fancies himself the patron saint of Earth's post-Meridian expansion and figures every man, woman, and child owes him obeisance."

"Rarified crowd. And here they are."

Barma took off his hat and sighed. "Yeah. Right outside city limits on my turf."

"And you called me."

"To say this one is complicated is like saying the platinum rock which got dropped in the desert a couple of hundred years ago shook the ground a little. I'm looking at the richest man in Seraph dead next to one of its biggest criminals, alongside the guy who calls the shots of the largest militia. This is going to cause a few ripples. And right now you're the only one I trust enough to eyeball this thing."

"Why me? You have an office of trained marshals."

"Yeah, the others are out. Plus, there isn't one of them who isn't at least a little tainted."

Miles straightened and ignored the complaints from his popping knees. "It happens. But it's the job and what you have to work with. What about the other agencies?"

"Yellow Tiger and Red District militias. And then there's Sheriff Vaca's office, but she just boomerangs everything that takes actual work over to the militias."

"From what I've seen, the militias handle calls outside the city when asked."

Barma gave him an appraising look. "Learn that from Captain Sin? I heard you two were dating."

"Three evenings out watching my son play what he calls music isn't dating."

"Whatever. My office has a specific mandate. Fugitives, court security, protect the mayor and city officials, and first response to major crimes outside of Seraph, from Devil's Bridge and points west and south out to 250 klicks. This one's a squeaker, but you're right. It's ours. Wishing it otherwise won't make it go away. I'm asking you for help."

"I already have a job."

As if on cue, Miles' device vibrated. A text from Tristan. "Dog keeps whining. ETA on your return?"

Miles swiped closed the notification. "Speaking of which, I need to get back."

"Quit. I can put you on the payroll as a deputized consultant."

"No, thanks. I did the cop thing for more years than I care to admit. The security gig pays the rent."

Barma's jaw tightened, and he nodded. Set his hat on his head and started texting. "Calling my forensic team out."

Miles studied the walls. Only a couple of burner holes in the steel. Not many misses. Laser pistols rarely penetrated a body. He walked carefully to the far end of the container where the heavy doors stood closed. Muddy footprints abounded, which he avoided. He pushed a door open. A small cul-de-sac lay at the end of an alley lined with more of the shipping crates. Two vehicles were parked in the dirt, one a polished black sedan and the other a Yellow Tiger desert runner.

"This is where they parked," Miles announced.

Barma didn't look up from his screen. "Saw it when I first arrived and checked for any survivors."

"Then you probably counted two vehicles here. Were any of the victims friends?"

"I'd guess they hated each other. This wasn't a social event."

"Yeah. That means either two of them carpooled, or one vehicle is missing."

Chapter Three

Miles followed Barma to the end of the muddy alley. They studied the ground together. From a cursory examination, three vehicles had recently entered, one had left.

"Maybe one of them got dropped off," Miles said.

"These three met here without bodyguards or assistants. None of them would have sat down with the others if anyone was breaking the rules. And I don't see them going for a nightcap or early breakfast after their meetup."

"So someone left. Could have been before the balloon went up. Who do the two cars belong to?"

Barma went back to the two vehicles. "Desert runner is Bing Patton's. Fancies himself a lawman rather than a company manager. Shotgun fell out of his hands. Drives his car around town on his own little patrols. It would be cute if he wasn't such a jackass."

Miles walked around the black sedan. Locked. The flashlight revealed a plush interior, with leather and silver trim and wood paneling on the dashboard. Insight identified the model. "Not a common make. Custom print job. Meridian manufacturer that went out of business over twenty years ago."

"Xander Trowbridge's. Usually has a driver and a string of secretaries at his side. Not tonight. And if he drove alone, so did everyone else."

"Maybe someone didn't follow the rules. Or the third car got stolen. Third body is Shahid Khar's? What did he drive?"

"Don't know. I've got a scan of the wheel marks. Hard to believe someone as paranoid as him left his car unlocked."

"Bad people do dumb things."

"Not Shahid."

"He showed up here, didn't he?"

Barma's device vibrated, and he took the call. "I'm at the scene right now." Pause. "I haven't requested any additional units yet." Another pause. "No, don't send them. We have a bad connection? I'm not releasing this scene to Red District or anyone else until my people finish their job."

The person on the other end of the line was loud enough for Miles to hear a woman's voice. She sounded firm and increasingly angry.

"I'll call this in when I'm ready. Don't—"

Barma looked as if he wanted to throw his phone.

"What was that?" Miles asked.

"Trouble. Sheriff's department heard about this somehow and they're sending their own investigators from the Red District militia."

"And you don't play nice with them?"

"Under normal circumstances, we get along swimmingly. But that was Sheriff Vaca herself on the line, and she's taken a personal interest. Which means the word is getting out about what happened here and it's going to get nasty."

Another text from Tristan. "Where r u? Dog won't leave. Shift's up in an hour and I need my car."

He put the phone away. "Who called you in the first place?"

"Yellow Tiger's dispatch program flagged Patton's runner outside of city limits and pinged my office. It's a nuisance call meant to dot the I's and cross the T's on our respective mandates. I was up and out. I called Bing. After receiving no reply, I checked it out."

"That'll teach you to go to bed at a reasonable hour."

"Not all of us can just plug in and recharge our batteries at the drop of a hat. Look, I have minutes before this place will be crawling with people I can't trust. Give me a day and help me run whatever leads we can. I'll make it worth your time. Once the militia shows up, I'll be up to my ears in phone calls and messages from the mayor on down and won't be able to get anything done. No one here knows you. You can ask the right questions and get things rolling by the time I have to loop any of my own people in."

It was exactly what Miles didn't want. To be seen, noticed, have his profile checked and investigated. The mystery woman from the train had helped wipe his presence clean from any other bounty hunters from Meridian who might pick up his scent.

"What's involved?" Miles asked. "I can give you a few hours, help with the scene, but beyond that, I can't get involved."

"I need to file a personnel form, adding you as a provisional deputy," Barma said. "We sometimes do that for folks we bring on board during operations requiring local help when out in the boonies. Sometimes we need to hire a tracker or impromptu backup."

"Can't we do this off the books?"

"Not with this. When the two militias hear about this and the Sheriff sends her own investigators, that's a lot of Seraph cops who are going to be throwing their weight around. If you're here, it's because you're official."

Can't? Won't. He had a job to return to.

Barma waited on Miles, expression calm, but eyes hopeful.

"I'll take a last look around," Miles said. "But then I have to leave."

Chapter Four

With spotlights blazing, a Red District armored car with oversized balloon tires drove down the alley. Steel scraped as it rubbed along one row of cargo containers. It stopped right behind the marshal service's lab tech buggy where his forensic man, dressed head to toe in a white plastic suit with goggles, was busy unloading equipment. The bumper of the armored car was emblazoned with red chevrons and threatened to shear the roof off the smaller vehicle.

The militia driver cut loose with a blast of a horn. "Get that car out of our way!"

As if there was any more room in the cul-de-sac. A militia trooper dropped to the dirt. and he and the forensic technician began arguing.

The flood lights and red and white flashers were blinding.

Miles was crouched, getting a scan of the tire tracks of the victims' vehicles. He squinted as he gazed at the new arrivals. "They always this subtle?"

Barma kept his back to the lights. True to his prediction, Barma had been answering a nonstop flurry of text messages. "It'll only get worse. Best make whatever observations you can before it gets crowded and you're asked to leave."

"I've seen what I need to. No other vehicles drove up here recently. Anything on Shahid's cars?"

"I've got Glenda on it back in the office. Just a sec."

More cops emerged from the armored car. A blonde woman in a blue windbreaker was the first to approach from the group. A visible implant wrapped around her left ear and adhered to her cheek and jawline.

Her tone was formal. "Marshal Barma, thanks for securing the scene. Please forward all your data to me now."

"My tech hasn't even gotten started. I'll call you when I can release this location."

"That won't be necessary. We're here now. Red District techs will handle processing and collect the bodies."

Miles brushed mud from his knees. "That's kinda quick. The marshal's tech hasn't even stepped foot inside."

She gave him a quick once-over. "What museum did you crawl from?"

"Military surplus. Seraph civil mandate places the marshal's office in charge of an investigation outside of city limits. Neither the Yellow Tigers nor the Red District militia are permitted to exercise their enforcement authority without approval by the sheriff's office or the marshal's."

Thanks, Insight.

Barma mouthed, "Shut up."

The cop in the windbreaker was grinning now. "I'm not sure who this is, Marshal Barma, but as you're escorting him away from this crime scene, please inform him that by my order, the Red District militia has assumed jurisdictional oversight and will handle this."

"And who are you?" Miles asked.

The woman ignored the question as she waved the Red District cops forward.

Miles held out a hand to stop the procession. "You realize your people are trampling all over the tire tracks leading to a crime scene."

The woman's grin vanished. She pivoted to face Miles. There was something snakelike in her movements, a serpent about to strike. "Marshal, get your people out of here now."

The marshal's office lab tech watched in obvious dismay. "Boss?"

"Pack it up," Barma said. He turned Miles towards the mouth of the alley. "You can get to your car this way."

"Wait a minute. What happened back there? Who is she?"

"She, my friend, is Sheriff Rose Vaca."

Insight had missed that. His Seraph net connection was suddenly too spotty to confirm the fact, but he didn't doubt what Barma told him. "Just like that, you get removed?"

"It's an open investigation. We just lost the crime scene. You gave me an hour and I appreciate it, but it's not your concern anymore."

"Are their people any good?"

"Depends. But what does it matter? You have your job to get back to."

"Someone drove away from this place, Barma, and the Red Banners just rolled over the wheel marks. We had people like your Sheriff Vaca up the chain of command back in River City. Bad things happen when cops start interfering like that."

"She can't take the case away from me," Barma said.

"But she can bully you from actually doing your job and solving it."

"Something like that."

Miles stopped them at the mouth of the alley. "How much?"

"How much what?"

"How much does working for the marshal department pay, if I give you a day, like you asked?"

Barma took out his device and pulled up a screen he had prepared. "There's the particulars."

"All right. I'll help. But promise me once we're done, you delete everything you have on me."

"What about your other job?"

"It'll keep. Besides, my watchman shift is almost over, and suddenly I'm not so tired."

Barma nodded and tapped his screen before offering it to Miles.

"Press there with your thumb, Kim. Welcome to the marshal service."

Chapter Five

Tristan was bouncing on his knees and shivering when Miles pulled up to the construction site's front gate. "What took you so long?"

The sun was rising. The first of the workers were gathering in the main lot, hard hats on, breath visible. Most gripped steaming cups of tea in their hands. The dog was nearby, sniffing about the cut section of gate.

Miles set the brake and got out of the wagon. "Marshal Barma had some consultation work."

"At three in the morning?"

"You want bank hours, work at a bank."

Tristan reached a hand over. "Whatever. I logged us out. I have your credit chip for the night. Now give me my keys, I need to get home."

Miles dropped them in his palm. "Barma has me running down some loose ends today. I could use a driver."

"I can't. Yasmin needs me back now. You know that."

"It couldn't hurt to ask. Just get me to my hotel."

The dog jumped in the back bed of the wagon.

"Hey!" Tristan shouted. "Get out! Go! Scram!"

The dog barked and wasn't going anywhere.

"It's going to get fleas in my tuk-tuk."

Miles appraised the dog. "At this point, it will only add to your car's character. Leave him be. I'll get him out once we make it to the hotel."

The dog jumped out once Miles stepped onto the curb. Tristan didn't wave as he sped off. The dog shrank back when Miles crouched and offered a hand but hurried to follow once Miles approached the hotel doors.

The clerk behind the plastic window glanced up from whatever serial he was watching on his tablet. "No animals. No exceptions."

"He's not mine."

"Then shut the door so it doesn't get in."

Miles reached for the door to hurry it closed. "Sorry, bud."

With the morning light outside, the dog's face was well illuminated. Its pink mouth had one corner which appeared scarred as if it was sneering. The animal whimpered as the door thudded closed, and a burst of hot breath fogged the glass.

"How much extra for you to let me take him in?" Miles asked.

"What, and have it barking and upsetting all the other tenants?"

"Hate for anyone to spoil the tranquil ambience, right?"

"Rent's due tomorrow. You said you get paid today."

Miles transferred the credits for the next week's stay to the waiting scanner at the front desk. There wasn't much left. He would need to hire a ride if he didn't want to begin his investigation on foot. His stomach reminded him he also needed breakfast.

He took the stairs and went up to his room. The clamor from his neighbors was in full swing: loud music and serials, thumps, footsteps, slammed doors, and voices through paper-thin walls. He needed a change of clothes but realized his extra shirt and sole change of underwear were still damp, drying near the bathroom sink.

The dog barked from outside. Miles glanced down through the window and saw it standing at the corner, glancing nervously about and whining.

In River City, they never had dogs or any other pets. Dillan had wanted one for years, but Seo Yeun had been adamant and worried an animal would cause allergies.

In reviewing the events at the murder scene, he wondered what he had been thinking in agreeing to help Barma. Was it the crime itself, the challenge, the thought someone needed his expertise? Or was it the Sheriff throwing her authority around?

What business did he have stepping into a new city and its problems, with its own rules which he couldn't begin to understand?

He'd help run down the missing witness's vehicle and bow out. His nagging stomach reminded him that the extra credits Barma threw his way would be welcome. He had enough for breakfast, maybe lunch, but if he wanted to get anywhere, he'd need to keep enough to hire a cab.

He washed his face and hands and ignored the reflection staring at him before pulling his hat back on. Once outside, the dog slinked over and followed him to the nearby drugstore where a selection of vending machines waited.

A moment later, he had a mint cereal bar and a scalding cup of tea-colored water. The dog stared with unvarnished cupidity. A string of drool dangled from its lips. Miles broke off a quarter of his bar, and the animal swallowed it in a single gulp.

"Chew your food, trooper," Miles said. "We can't have you choking to death in the mess. It's the enemy's job to kill you. Your job is to make it harder for him."

His phone buzzed. Message from Barma. "Glenda sent me this. Let me know if it helps."

He ate as he read. Surprisingly moist bar, nutty, too sweet. At least the grumblies subsided. The tea had cooled some but was still too hot.

The first attachment was a spec sheet on a style of four-wheel roadster. It matched the wheelbase measurement of the tire tracks from the crime scene. A second attachment held a map of Seraph. Some thirty virtual pins adorned the map, all addresses or locations in town where a roadster had been spotted by traffic patrols. The image had a Yellow Tiger watermark. Miles could only speculate if the militia was always so sharing with the marshal.

Most of the locations were downtown, but half were spread around the city. Too many districts had no marks, which meant either that no roadsters of that make had passed near a camera, or that street and patrol surveillance were lacking. A list of owners would have been better, but Miles guessed this was something a city official like the sheriff would have, and either Barma didn't have access or didn't want to ask.

Incomplete information. The locations were a long shot. All of this would be toe work handled by a few mobile units who could eyeball each pin as quickly as possible. Vehicles moved around. But a lead was a lead, and he had thumbed his agreement to help.

With Tristan off playing father for the day, Miles needed to secure a ride. A moment on Seraph net was a sobering realization that taxis were expensive.

Dillan picked up on the second ring. "Hey, dad. What's up?"

"I know you're probably getting ready for work. I need a lift."

"Not a good day for that. I'm already late. I thought I told you I have a show we're working on with the kids. I have to be down at the theater in...look, I have to go—just a sec."

At first, Miles thought Dillan had hung up. A muffled conversation followed on the other end. Dillan and his girlfriend Zoe. His son sounded a bit upset.

Dillan returned. "Dad, you at your hotel?"

"I'm just outside."

"All right. Look, I can't get you. But Zoe has wanted to meet you. She said she'll be there in twenty minutes."

As Miles waited, he checked his reflection in the polished surface of one of the vending machines. His hair felt greasy, but at least his face was free of grime. Not much helping the rest of it at this point.

Zoe pulled up moments later in a two-door electric super-mini. Miles recognized her from a picture Dillan had shared, as she had been absent from Dillan's performances, always working, according to Dillan.

She had a headful of locks tucked into a scrunchy, which kept it all up and off her neck and out of her face. She rolled down the windows and leaned against the wheel to look at Miles. "You must be Dillan's father. I'm Zoe."

"Miles," he said as he climbed in. The dog, which had been nearby sniffing the vending machines, had vanished. "Thanks for coming. I hope this isn't an inconvenience."

"I just dropped Dillan off. Sorry, he's really stressed about his kids' show. The school is making it into a bigger production than he hoped."

"A fundraiser, he told me."

"Yeah. Good cause. Some of the schools where the kids go are volunteering their best students. He's got thirty kids to corral, songs, a couple of dance numbers. There's other classes doing stuff too, but he kept saying yes."

"Story of my life. Look, I appreciate this. I just need to get downtown. I have a job."

She put the car in gear. "Oh? What are you working on? I heard you had a night security gig."

"I do. But I agreed to help the marshal out with something that came up last night."

"The marshal? This have to do with the train incident?"

"No. There was a murder."

Chapter Six

An interrogation. That's what it was. Not a chat, not a conversation, but an interrogation, and Miles had been grilled by the best of them. Meridian defense attorneys, judges, and victim rights advocates could take a lesson from Zoe Franklin.

As the questions flew, she drove him to twelve of the locations where a matching roadster had been sighted by the Seraph traffic scanners. Only three still had cars parked. With all three, Miles got out and made a cursory examination.

Most vehicles in town had a stenciled tag number on a corner of the bumper, a city use permit which no doubt paid for Seraph infrastructure.

He texted each car's number to Barma. A moment later, he was looking at a profile of the owner: name, address, picture. Barma could keep track of these and follow up. Just because a car was at a murder scene didn't mean it had been the registered owner who had driven it. But it would be a direction to go.

In this case, Barbara Zwick was an elderly woman who owned a nearby ceramic studio. Low on the list of suspects, and the roadster was in plain sight. The previous two were also unlikely candidates: a nurse at Wood Creek hospital who worked day shift postnatal care, and a father of four who ran a foster care home with his partner.

Once he got back into Zoe's car, the inquisition resumed.

"Why did you finally decide to leave River City?" Zoe asked. And "Tell me about Dillan's mom." Followed by, "I heard you got to meet Beatrix Fish. Is she as weird as everyone says?"

Finally, she inquired, "What brought you to Seraph in the first place?"

A simple question with a simple answer, which would have avoided telling her anything about his original intention to sell off his cybernetics to a black-market surgeon and forward the proceeds to Dillan. But she had sniffed out something, perhaps his tiniest hesitation before his answer.

"This is where my son lives."

She leaned on the steering wheel, her eyes fixed on him. "It took you two years to come visit. No call, no message, and you were just going to show up?"

"I thought if I made contact first, he'd tell me not to come. Or I'd change my mind."

"So you jumped on the fastest train to Seraph. That's commitment. Not cheap, either. Did you come into a windfall?"

"Pull around there. The next car spotted was in the lot behind the restaurant."

She did as he requested, driving up towards several cars parked in a dirt lot.

No roadster.

Miles knew the list might be nothing but busy work. The real investigation was with the three bodies out beyond Bright Blocks where the fallen victims had met. Something in the diverse lives of a militia company executive, a water baron, and an underworld data broker brought them together in the small hours without staff or bodyguards. And while someone had driven off, that person no doubt had their vehicle stashed away where no traffic camera could spot it.

Still, the low-level grunt work occasionally bore fruit. And it nagged at him that Sheriff Vaca and the Red Banner militia had so carelessly obliterated the tire tracks. What else would they miss in their haste to make the crime scene go away? Above his pay grade. He could only hope Marshal Barma would ask the right questions.

"No car here, Miles," Zoe said. "So how much pension does a retired Meridian cop pull in, anyway?"

"Kind of a personal question."

"I'm trying to learn the lay of the land with Dillan. He doesn't share much, and what he does tell me doesn't come easy. It's like pulling teeth."

"Why is my financial situation so interesting?"

"You pay for an expensive train ticket rather than the long loop on a cheap bus. But then you stay in a Gallina Road dive. And no offense, but you look like you haven't changed clothes in a few days. Did you lose your luggage?"

He had brought none. He hadn't been planning on living more than a few hours after his arrival in Seraph. The train ride? Prior to the ambush, it would have brought him to his destination the quickest with the least chance of him being caught by anyone from Meridian who might be chasing him. After all, his implants weren't exactly his.

He gave her his winningest smile. "Maybe we would know each other better if you weren't skipping out on the evenings of Dillan's performances."

Her cheerful expression didn't waver. "I know! It's terrible. But I've hit a busy patch with work. I'm trying to finish my thesis, and night is the only time when everyone is out of the office and greenhouses so I can think clearly and get some dictation done."

"I thought Dillan said you were a farmer."

"Hah. It's what I told him when we first met. I'm a botanist. Right now I'm trying to revive some lost species of hops in my company's greenhouse. It's not super interesting, so I won't bore you."

"Well, this has been a big help. You can drop me off here. I can walk to the rest of my stops."

"You kidding me? It's hot out. And I need the break. Maybe I can take you to lunch before we part ways. But then how will you get around?"

Miles had considered the possibilities. Even a pedal bike was too expensive. And until the credits started rolling in, he couldn't afford to lose his room, and he wanted to stretch out his meal budget.

"I'll manage. I have another stop over by—pull over."

Zoe had already left the lot. She swerved and found a place to park on the street. A row of parking spaces lined the far side of the lot next to a neighboring building. A black roadster sat in one spot.

"What do you see?" Zoe asked.

"One of the vehicles I'm looking for. It must not have been there for the last traffic patrol update."

"Want me to get out and get the number for you?"

"Stay here."

Miles took a walk. He didn't have to get close for the number. But something about the car stood out. There was other foot traffic and he didn't want to linger, so he strolled past to the front of the building. A hair salon, a burrito shop, and a law office shared the property. Miles glanced at the directory information for the law office.

Svetlana Petroff Associates. No hours. No scan code for a phone number. The reflective glass didn't allow Miles to see inside. And above the door was a tiny camera. Miles kept moving, crossing the street and making his way back to Zoe.

She had a lecture playing. German language. Insight couldn't keep up as the play speed was double. She paused it. "Sorry. A little homework."

"It's your car."

"Any clues?"

"Possibly. Car parked at a law office. Might not be connected. But there's something about this roadster. I notice most cars around here have a nice layer of dust on them."

"Including mine. Sticks to everything, and water's expensive."

"Yeah. That one's been washed, probably this morning. Crime scene was muddy."

He sent the car's number to Barma. Again, a fast answer. Perhaps the marshal had Miles tied into the office's computer. On his screen he saw a boyish face, a man in his early twenties, neutral expression, the kind you see on a license. Bristly black hair. Rust-colored eyes. Lucien Khar. Address was near downtown. No other information.

Zoe was reading over his arm. "Khar family? Was one of them involved?"

Miles studied Lucien's face on the screen. Like so many mugshots, there was no knowing what might lurk behind those gentle eyes and his youthful face.

"It's too much of a coincidence. Yes, I think this is the roadster I was looking for. Zoe, you've been great. But it's time for me to let you get on with your day."

"You kidding me? This is the most excitement I've seen in maybe ever."

Miles moved his hand in front of the vent spewing cool air. "Too much excitement. I'm calling Barma and handing this off to him. Then we're both done with this."

The call to Barma went to voice mail. Miles sent a text, called again, and hung up. Watched the parking lot and the sidewalk in the passenger-side mirror.

"So you grow hops," Miles prompted.

"Primarily research into lost varieties and coming up with new tweaked clones that will do well here. There're incentives from River City and New Pacific. People want their beer. Foundation of any civilized culture."

"If you say so."

"Not a fan?"

"I don't drink. It makes my face go flush."

She laughed but stopped herself. "I can't tell when you're joking."

"Most people have that problem."

Two people emerged from the law office. One was a husky woman in a suit and tie. She was pursuing a younger man. Miles zoomed in. Lucien Khar. He was dressed in a bright blue untucked button-down shirt, walking fast, and purposefully ignoring the woman on his heels. He made it to the roadster before holding out his hand, palm up. The woman, Svetlana Petroff, or one of the associates, Miles guessed, reached into a pocket and handed over a set of keys. She wasn't done with whatever imploring protest but got out of the way when Lucien climbed into the roadster.

"Start the car," Miles said.

Zoe turned the key, and the electric engine purred to life. Lucien was backing out. He left the attorney in a cloud of chalky dust as he sped off.

Zoe followed. "Don't get to do this often while watching plants grow."

Chapter Seven

Lucien drove fast.

As Miles hung on and Zoe put the pedal down, they were heading into the heavier traffic of central Seraph. If Lucien was fearful after the night's events, he didn't show it by his driving. He weaved in and out of lanes, cutting off trucks and almost clipping a hapless robot delivery dog. Miles guessed he might be heading home. But Lucien took a northbound lane to leave the downtown area and was soon driving through a commercial district, which Insight marked as being close to Seraph's university.

Zoe hung back like a pro, keeping a few cars between them and never trying to match Lucien's speed. There was always enough traffic that she could almost catch up. But then a two-trailer truck got in the way. Zoe had to maneuver into a turn lane. As soon as she sped up, she slammed on the brakes.

A light flashed red. A group of pedestrians began crossing.

Miles kept quiet, scanning the street for a glimpse of the roadster. Where had it gone?

By the time the signal changed and the last half-dozen pedestrians moved unhurriedly out of the crosswalk, Zoe had to wait for the truck to precede them before pulling back onto the street.

"I'm sorry," she said. "I lost him."

"Relax. You're not supposed to be doing any of this. You need to drop me off up ahead at the corner. I'll continue on foot. It's my job, not yours—hey!"

She drove past the corner and kept going.

"Zoe..."

"It's my car. You want me to find him with or without you?"

The main drag was a large loop which passed a set of decorative gates. University of Seraph, the scrolling ironwork read. More pedestrians moved about. Students, Miles realized. They endured another long light as a mostly young crowd crossed the road.

Miles scanned the faces. "This your alma mater?"

"Yup. It's either here or a virtual school unless you want to travel back to River City or out to New Pacific."

They chugged along with the flow of traffic, the university grounds on one side and dorms, auxiliary school buildings, and businesses on the other. Soon, the avenue ahead veered off. It wasn't a complete loop. No roadster in sight.

"Keep going?" Zoe asked.

"Turn around. I don't think he'd come this way if he was in a hurry."

"You a pro on Seraph traffic patterns?"

"Cars are in my DNA."

On the return trip, Miles studied the parking lots as they passed. Unlike River City, everything was spread out, with only a few raised or underground parking structures once you got away from downtown. Bad for sprawl, good for his current search.

"There."

A narrow lot with a dozen filled spaces lay sandwiched between an administration building and an eatery. The roadster was nestled by a No Parking sign.

Zoe waited for a van to leave a spot on the street. "This place is good. Fresh bread, soups, beer."

"No. If you're sticking around, you're waiting out here."

"Or what?"

"No 'or what.' This guy might be complicit in a murder and might have had a hand in it."

"So call the marshal."

"That's what I'm going to do. I'm also going to walk in there and see if I can spot him. The way he's speeding around, he might be looking to slip away."

Zoe made a show of her hands off the wheel before clicking play on her lecture. Miles got out and headed for the eatery.

Plants in terra-cotta pots lined the entry, and a misting fan blew cool water down at an outside sitting area. The air felt balmy. The place was full, both outside and in for what should have been an early lunch crowd. But the eatery served breakfast, judging by the chalkboard specials list and the plates of egg dishes and baked goods. A young crowd had steaming cups of tea or chicory and spoke through mouthfuls of pancakes and soy sausage. Some read or were working on their tablets. A bar served beer, but only a few were partaking. A muted cricket match played on a large screen near the bar.

Miles was the only one wearing a hat. He took it off as he surveyed the restaurant.

Herbaceous aromas mixed with the thick smell of cooked meat, or a near perfect facsimile. Too many scented soaps and deodorants. Insight began identifying the languages spoken: English, Mandarin, Russian, Hebrew, Finnish, Arabic.

"Shut up, Insight."

A perky server with pigtails and triple studs through the bridge of her nose approached him. "There's a spot at the bar, or it's a fifteen-minute wait."

"Bar's fine."

Minutes later, he was the only one drinking hot tea at the bar, but no one paid him any mind. A pair of kids sharing a tome-sized tablet kept bumping him as they watched an animated video with bouncy music playing so loud that it competed with the buzz of the crowd. They both looked young enough to still be in primary school, but both had half-finished lagers.

He endured another bump just as he was about to chance a sip of his steaming beverage. Decided to set it down lest he require more skin grafts.

Took in the hairstyles, clothing, makeup, piercings, body language, and group dynamics.

Bright colors were in, as were bare shoulders and plunging necklines and long sleeves. The crowd had a sameness to it despite the endless variety. But each group had its loudest dresser. Loudest talker, too, and the competition was ongoing. People flirted, bragged, spoke with their mouths full, and shouted over one another. And like islands in a fast-moving stream, there were solitary diners with earphones oblivious to it all, eating or studying, alone yet together.

Bump.

The waitstaff proved efficient in delivering food and drink, and every empty table was quickly filled with more patrons. Miles wondered if school was actually in session.

Bump.

Miles had surveyed most of the restaurant except for the patio. A large group occupying a corner booth was partially obscured by a partition. They didn't have any turnover. A girl was reading from a tablet and, unlike the rest of the larger groups, everyone at the table was quiet and listening intently. The back of one head looked like Lucien. Black, short, cropped hair. He wore a charcoal tank top and was lean and muscled. From Miles' angle, it was impossible to confirm it was him. But then he stood, and Miles saw the blue shirt wrapped around his waist.

Lucien Khar began reading from the tablet. The table sat intently and listened.

Bump.

Miles adjusted his stool, edging away, but his neighbors occupied the void in moments.

Miles poked the nearest kid whose butt kept nudging him. The young woman looked at him for a moment before doing a double take.

"Do you mind?" Miles asked.

The girl appeared ready to give a retort but edged away. The pair resumed their viewing of what turned out to be footage of a video game match. The two were now violating the airspace of a couple of women sharing the same glass of beer and holding hands.

"Hey!" one woman said after her first bump.

Miles knew he couldn't save everyone. He returned his attention to Lucien. Texted Barma. After a minute without a reply, Miles got up and approached the table. He realized Lucien was reading lines of dialogue with two of the women at the table.

"Let's stop there," said a woman of about thirty wearing a maroon blazer. "That's perfect, Lucien. You get Garcin. We still need to vote on who we'd like to play Estelle."

"It's obvious," a girl in a checkered scarf said. "Tilly nailed it."

Another of the students raised a finger. "I preferred Sophie. Estelle should be a snot, you know? After all, she's a murderer."

A murmur of agreement followed.

Lucien hadn't sat down. "I'd like to hear Sophie as Inez. And with all respect to Tilly, I vote for Li to play Estelle. She has the voice and bearing."

The woman in the maroon blazer licked her lips. "But Li is first year. She's on stage duty. She can understudy with Tilly."

"No. Li it is. She's perfect. Let's do a read around with Li and Sophie. You'll see I'm right."

A moment of silence followed. The table appeared to be waiting for the woman in the blazer.

"Of course. Let's resume this evening at the theater. Maybe hearing everyone's lines in the auditorium will affect our decision."

Miles had taken a position near the partition and an emergency exit. No one had noticed him as the group gathered their belongings. Two of the other students lingered as the others departed, and Lucien settled in again with the tablet and began reading. He didn't look like someone on the run or ready to bolt, and Miles was in no mood to chase someone down.

He sent a message to Barma. "Lucien Khar is at Green Moon Café. Saw car. Good chance he was at scene last night."

Miles waited a moment without receiving a reply. As the space cleared before him, he took the opportunity and slid into the booth. "You're Lucien Khar."

Lucien glanced up but appeared unfazed by Miles' appearance. "I don't know you. This is a private table."

"Isn't this the theater group?"

"We're with Mr. McKenzie's advanced class," one of the two remaining students offered helpfully.

"You're no student," Lucien said.

Miles showed his hands and shrugged. "Guilty. I do need to talk to Lucien. It's a sensitive matter. You two don't mind, do you?"

The two students scooted out of the booth. "See you later, Lucien," one said.

Lucien had put his tablet away and pushed his chair back as if to leave.

"I wouldn't go just yet," Miles said. "Right now this is a friendly conversation."

"Implying it won't be if I don't cooperate?"

The kid was cool. Young man, really, judging by the age, but the tone was that of a much younger teenager.

"I'm not implying anything. But I might make things go easier for you. You were there last night out in the junkyard past Bright Blocks."

"I don't know what you're talking about. You don't look like a cop."

"Your car was there. It's only a matter of time before someone finds a trace of something to mark your presence: a fingerprint, a smudge on your clothes, a shoe mark. I served as a police officer with the Meridian military. You bring that lawyer of yours with you, you say what you did and what you saw, it goes better for you."

Lucien kept a neutral expression while locking eyes with Miles. "You're here out of the kindness of your heart to get me to turn myself in for some unknown crime? Sounds like you're fishing."

"It has something to do with your father."

Still no reaction. "You don't look like someone who knows my dad except maybe what you read in the news feed. So take your shakedown and stuff it before I call the militia and tell them you're harassing me."

Was this the face of someone who had seen his father gunned down that morning?

Lucien got up. When Miles also stood, the young man grasped a necklace with a small button attached. "One push, and my security team shows up."

Miles made a show of keeping his hands flat on the table. "I'm here to help you, believe it or not."

But Lucien wasn't sticking around to prolong the conversation. He navigated his way past the waitstaff and headed for the door. Miles followed. Checked his device and confirmed no response from Barma. If the marshal wanted what might be the best witness and suspect to the night's main event, he'd need to show up quick.

Outside, a man in overalls was busy with a toolbox near the roadster. He appeared to be digging through it as if searching for the right wrench or screwdriver. But he looked straight at Lucien when he emerged from the eatery doors. Lucien marched towards his car, oblivious. Miles moved to catch up, grabbing one of several stanchions meant to direct customers out of the path of parking cars, but the rope was missing.

Lucien turned to face Miles. At the same time, the man in overalls pulled a boxy pistol from the toolbox. Raised it.

Miles charged. "Get down!"

The pistol went off as Miles shoved past Lucien and swung the stanchion. The heavy base caught the man across the side of the head. He fell, the weapon tumbling. But the man recovered quickly, reaching for the pistol. Miles smashed the stanchion down on his hand. The man screamed and tightened up into a ball.

Where was Lucien?

At the lot's entrance, Lucien was running, passing between the cars parked outside and across the street. He had his hand on his necklace and was squeezing the alarm. No sound, but the panic button was no doubt calling for help.

Miles grabbed the dropped weapon. Not a burner. A dart gun? "Get back here!" he shouted as he ran.

Lucien stopped halfway across the street. A militia cruiser with red markings cut loose with a *WHUP!* from its siren as it flashed its light bar. Lucien changed direction. Sprinting now. Traffic swerved to avoid him.

A cop on a loudspeaker shouted, "Stop right there!"

Miles was on Lucien's heels when Zoe sprang out of her car and got in Lucien's way. They collided. As they went down to the concrete, Lucien was swearing and trying to get her to let go.

Miles grabbed Lucien and held him down. "It's all right, I got him."

One cop was running their way. Miles set the weapon down while keeping his weight on the wriggling young man.

"Both hands up," the cop ordered. "Let me see your hands." He had his pistol out, a compact needle thrower.

"I'm Miles Kim. I'm with the marshal's office. This is our suspect."

The cop's attention was divided between Miles and Zoe, who had gotten up and now stood stiffly with her arms in the air. "Down on the ground."

His helmet mike blathered. The driver who had been on the loud-speaker was out of the cruiser.

"Call backup and the wagon. Tell station we have Lucien Khar in custody. Get the—"

Something struck the cop, and he tumbled. The side window of the militia cruiser shattered. The driver took cover. Miles grabbed Zoe and shoved her down against her car. He kept his head down. The cop had a dart imbedded into his back. It had pierced his armor.

The other cop began shooting, but at what, Miles couldn't tell. The *spat-spat-spat* of the needle pistol was a dull cough. Miles opened the door to the vehicle and pushed Zoe inside.

"Keep your head down. Start the car."

He seized Lucien and pulled him up from the ground. Lucien didn't struggle as they scurried around the front of the vehicle and into the passenger side. It was cramped, and Miles accidentally slammed the door on Lucien's foot before getting him completely in.

"Go! Drive!"

"Where?" Zoe shouted, her voice cracking.

"Anywhere but here!"

She got the car in gear and floored it. Miles winced at the thought someone might shoot at them as he raised his head. No one blocking the road in front of them. And behind was a snarl of vehicles. The militia cruiser was out of sight.

Zoe was breathing fast as she swerved through traffic.

Miles put a hand on hers. "We're okay. Slow down. We don't want to crash."

She nodded, but she only drove faster as they hit an open lane.

"Get off me," Lucien groaned.

Miles did his best to adjust himself. But he wasn't taking chances and didn't want to stop so they could get comfortable.

"What was that? Who's shooting?" Zoe asked.

"I don't know. Militia was after him, but someone else was too, and there was more than one of them."

"Intersection coming up. Which way?"

Any direction. Pick one.

But that was panicked thinking. Insight reminded him of where they were, and he had a location in mind once he forced his brain to calm down.

"Marshal's office. We're heading to the marshal's office. Take a right up ahead."

Zoe took the turn, straining the limits of her compact car.

"All right," Miles said, "You're doing good. We got away. Take it easy."

She eased off the accelerator. Hiccuped. Glanced nervously at Miles and the other passenger. "Are we still in danger?"

"Not for the moment. I'm getting us someplace safe and then getting you home."

She wiped sweat from her eyes. Blinked and focused on the road. "That...sounds good."

"Are you hurt?"

She shook her head. Miles checked himself for any injuries, and then patted Lucien down as best he could. No one appeared to be following them.

"Pull over," Lucien groaned. "Let me out."

"Not a chance. Pipe down. Zoe, stay in this lane."

"I know where I'm going." She drank from a water bottle. The hiccups continued without letup. "Things like this happen to you often?"

"You just picked a crazy day to say yes to giving me a ride. Is this enough excitement for you?"

Chapter Eight

The unblinking red eye stared down at them.

They waited in the marshal's office entry, a short hallway surrounded by one-way glass. The red eye stood above the second door which led inside, and it was attached to a black metal form which might hold an assortment of defensive measures.

"Get Barma on the line," Miles said for the third time into the com box mounted on the wall.

But Glenda, the woman on the other end of the box, wasn't answering. She had told them to wait, and that had been it.

Zoe stood next to him, hugging her elbows and looking pasty. Miles could empathize. Throwing up was perfectly natural after being shot at. He kept one hand on Lucien. The young man kept quiet, his jaw tight, his eyes taking in everything.

Miles went to the door and started banging with his metal hand.

"Stop it," Glenda called from the box.

"Then let us in. Barma signed me on to help as a temporary deputy. I have a witness for him, and someone's already tried to snatch him once."

He glanced back through the door to the street. No one outside. But that could change any moment. He second-guessed his decision to bring Zoe and Lucien to the marshal's. Should have cut Zoe loose. But her face and her vehicle had been seen by the militia and whoever else was trying to get Lucien, so she wasn't safe out on the street. Not that standing around in a glass room was much better.

Miles prepared to resume pounding when the door clicked and

popped open. He shoved Lucien along as Zoe followed. The cool air was a welcome relief from the heat.

Glenda wasn't smiling. But Miles had never seen her do anything but glower. The tense diminutive woman wore a badge pinned to a white button-down shirt and a sidearm clipped to her belt. She conducted them past several desks to a side room with benches, a row of lockers, a kitchen counter with a sink, and a pair of cells with bars. The office was empty besides them.

"Where is everyone?" Miles asked.

"Out." Glenda held out her hand. "I'll take that gun."

He handed it over without comment.

"Stay in here. Bathroom's through that door, otherwise don't wander."

Miles followed her when she turned to leave.

"Did I not make myself clear?" she asked.

"Hear anything from Marshal Barma?"

"No. And I don't have any record of you as a new hire. Back in the waiting room."

"So why did you let us in?"

"Because deputizing someone without clearing it with me sounds like something he'd do."

Glenda waited. Stared. Miles returned to the waiting room. Lucien was pacing. Zoe was texting, her fingers a flurry, but she appeared to be constantly deleting whatever she had written.

"You can't keep me a prisoner," Lucien said miserably. "I didn't do anything."

"You haven't told me otherwise. I'm not making any accusations. What happened last night?"

"You almost got me killed back there."

"I saved your ass. Did you recognize that man?"

Lucien shook his head.

"I searched for you on behalf of Marshal Barma. But the guy by your car wasn't trying to bring you in for polite questioning. Stun dart, I'd guess, and he had a friend, or friends, and they were willing to shoot at militia to get to you."

"And you want me to believe you're on my side?"

"Think what you want. I didn't come at you guns blazing. I believe you were at a meeting last night where things went very badly. One of the victims was your father, and you saw what happened. You visited your lawyer this morning, got your car cleaned up, and then went to meet your theater group like it was a normal school day. Now take off your shoes."

"What?"

"You heard me. Take them off, or I take them off for you."

Miles watched as Lucien sat on a bench and pulled off his loafers. He had flecks of mud on the bottom of his slacks. The loafers weren't clean. All Miles needed was an analysis machine and a sample of the soil and mud near the shipping containers. It would confirm Lucien's presence. As certain as a fingerprint. But before Miles could touch the shoes, voices came from the front of the office.

Sheriff Vaca, and she was arguing with Glenda.

"I don't care. Bring him out here," Vaca said.

It took Miles a moment to realize she was speaking through the entry lobby call box. He moved from the waiting room into the main office. Vaca was on Glenda's desktop monitor, looking up at the camera. The fisheye lens warped her face and shoulders, turning her into a grotesque monstrosity.

"I can't do that, Sheriff Vaca," Glenda said. "Your authority ends once you step through that door. I didn't write the rules, but I enforce them in this office."

"Lucien Khar is a witness to a murder, and his life is in danger."

"So what safer place than here?"

"I've assigned Red District to the investigation. That means your office is no longer lead on this. Lucien is our witness, and I need him. If the marshal was here, he'd agree with me."

"Well, he isn't, is he, dearie? I have Lucien tagged and logged as one of *our* witnesses. When Marshal Barma returns, you can settle this."

Glenda's stock was rising in Miles' book.

"Who else is here that I can speak to?" Vaca asked.

"Everyone else is out."

"Okay, I get it. You don't make the rules. Then let me in. I need to talk to him."

Glenda leaned back from the keyboard. Muted, the screen said. Her eyes narrowed when she saw Miles. "I thought I told you to stay put."

He pointed to Vaca's image on the screen. "You trust her?"

"Honey, I don't get paid to trust anyone."

"If she comes in, will you let me stay with Lucien for any interrogation?"

"I wasn't planning on letting her in."

"I've got the kid's shoes, which need soil trace analysis. You can do that here, can't you?"

"Of course."

"Let her in. Take the shoes. Run the tests while we talk."

She studied him for a moment before unmuting her microphone. "Okay, Sheriff, come on in. Check any weapon with me, then you'll get your interview."

Chapter Nine

"Where are his shoes?" Sheriff Vaca asked.

She stood in the hallway outside of the interview room Glenda had chosen for them. Miles walked Lucien past her, a guiding hand on his arm. Zoe remained in the waiting room. She was on the phone with Dillan. From the snippets of conversation, Miles' son didn't sound happy.

"I asked you a question." Vaca followed them into the room. It felt like a large closet, with plastic chairs and a small table fixed to a wall.

"He took them," Lucien said as Miles sat him in the far chair.

Miles leaned on the wall by the door. "Old Meridian trick. No shoes, folks tend to calm down and not try to go anywhere they're not supposed to."

"That's the stupidest thing I've heard," Vaca said as she sat opposite Lucien. "You can go now, Mr. Kim."

"You must have missed our introduction this morning. Marshal Barma brought me on to consult with this investigation."

"I don't have your paperwork. You're no marshal."

"You either take my word for it, or I remind you we're both guests here."

Vaca leaned as if searching for Glenda. But she was nowhere to be found. Miles had seen her enter the waiting room and hopefully was taking the shoes to be tested. Lucien's prints would be helpful too, along with a hair sample and skin scrape.

Vaca blinked hard. No doubt activating her implants. "Lucien Khar,

I'm Sheriff Rose Vaca. Do you currently need any medical assistance before we begin this interview?"

"I'm feeling fine," he said.

"How about I have the temporary deputy marshal bring you a cup of tea?"

"Ask your questions."

"Your father Shahid Khar was murdered last night along with two others."

Lucien was staring at the table and tracing a pattern with a finger. His fingernails were buffed and polished. "Are you looking for confirmation, Sheriff? I thought that would be the coroner's job."

"I'm telling you your father's dead, and you're making a joke?"

"No joke. And I already heard about my father."

"From who?"

"My lawyer."

Vaca blinked hard. "Svetlana Petroff. Do you know how she heard?"

Lucien shrugged. "Ask her."

Miles suppressed a grin. He knew the tough nut act when he saw it. Sometimes meant the witness or suspect had something to hide. Also, could be they had a reason to be so smug. Or they hated cops.

"Were you close with your father?"

"I'm still processing the news. I'm gutted," Lucien said flatly. "How much longer will we be?"

"As long as we need. I understand there was an attempt on your life this morning."

"I don't know what happened. Miles Kim here saved me."

"Did you have a relationship with Mr. Kim prior to today?"

"Never seen him before. Maybe you need to ask him some of your hard-hitting questions."

"I'm talking to you right now. Can you account for your activities last night?"

The entryway door buzzed. Lucien glanced up, apparently eager to see who might be coming. Miles looked out into the hallway.

Marshal Barma marched towards them, Glenda hot on his heels.

"Sheriff Vaca?" his voice boomed. "Why are you interviewing a person of interest in my station?"

"Let it be known that Marshal Barma has now joined us," Vaca said to no one. "Marshal, I sent you several messages since we last saw each other this morning. You haven't replied to any of them."

"My device wasn't working."

"Yet somehow you show up when Lucien Khar gets brought in."

"I don't care if you believe me or not," Barma said. "This is inappropriate. You have the crime scene, but my office is still conducting its investigation. Red District has shared none of its findings yet. You're upset at *me* for withholding information?"

"Yes. I decide who investigates what. And you've brought in outside help on a very sensitive event. I'm questioning your professionalism."

"Miles Kim is a deputized consultant and none of your concern."

Miles smiled and waved two fingers at the sheriff.

She said, "I'm directing you to release Lucien to my custody and for your 'consultant' to deliver all images and files associated with last night's event."

"You'll need an order from the mayor."

A grin split her face. A hard blink, and Barma's phone pinged. He checked his device and his jaw clenched.

"Looks like your phone is working again," the sheriff said. "Everything in order?"

Barma was reading and scrolling.

"Good," she said. "Lucien is coming with me. Mr. Kim, please find me his shoes."

The front door buzzed again.

"By the saints, now what?" Glenda said.

A brief exchange on the intercom was followed by the loud footsteps of shoes with heels. Svetlana Petroff appeared with two men in dark suits at her side. She wore dark glasses and a different suit than before, this one teal with a black houndstooth pattern.

"Weapons?" Glenda asked.

Svetlana touched her sunglasses and the lenses went clear. "None of my associates brought sidearms into the marshal's office. Marshal Barma? Sheriff Vaca? Unless you're placing my client under arrest, I'm ending this interview. He just lost his father, and now you're holding him here and asking him questions without me present?"

"He didn't request his lawyer," Vaca said.

Svetlana gave her an are-you-serious look before slipping past everyone. "I'll expect a formal request for my client's presence to come to me first. Come on, Lucien. We're going."

"Took you long enough," Lucien grumbled.

"Wait," Miles said. "He had people come after him by the school."

"People?" Svetlana asked. "What people?"

"I don't know. Man in overalls, another shooter. An attempted abduction, I'm guessing."

"Then I'll be sure to double his protection detail. If you want to schedule an interview with him, call my office. Lucien, where are your shoes?"

Svetlana, along with the two bodyguards, escorted Lucien out of the station. Sheriff Vaca lingered for a moment, sending a few messages before likewise departing. Glenda went to her desk, leaving Barma and Miles standing in the hallway. Zoe waited in the doorway to the waiting room. Miles motioned for her to stay put.

"What just happened?" Miles asked.

Barma slipped his device into his pocket and dabbed his sweaty brow with a handkerchief. "Delayed it for as long as possible. But the sheriff has the case, and she can delegate it to whomever she pleases. Mayor's approval, so I have no choice."

"That stunt with your phone never worked in my day."

"It still doesn't today. She'll make me pay for that."

"So what did you learn?"

"Less than I hoped. Talked to your girlfriend Captain Sin. Yellow Tigers are just learning about what happened to Bing Patton. They're having an emergency board of directors meeting right now. Sin talked to his secretary, his ex-wife, and all her officers. No one knew he had anything planned last night. And Xander Trowbridge gave his bodyguard the evening off. Seems Shahid's the only one who brought a plus-one to the party. Kid say anything?"

"The kid went to his lawyer this morning. His car got cleaned, but I didn't have time to check it myself. Glenda had a few minutes with his shoes. Might get something there. But Lucien Khar spent the rest of his day with his drama group at the university and barely seems to register his father got gunned down. And then, after we got attacked, he shrugged it off like nothing had happened. He's a cool fish."

"Shock will do that."

"So will a guilty conscience. But I don't know if he was an active participant in the junkyard shooting. He's no saint, but if he was there, he kept his hands clean. Literally."

Barma grumbled. "Huh. Unless he got himself tidied up, head to toe. I'll check on the samples from the shoes. But you heard the sheriff. This office is done."

"Are you?"

"Used to be two departments here who shared enforcement duties and police work. Marshals and sheriff. Then the city fathers hired out instead of expanding what we had. Enter the militias. Couple of small companies at first just for traffic and routine law and order duty. Then some of those started merging into what we have now."

"Red Banners and Yellow Tigers," Miles said.

"Yeah. There are a couple of smaller outfits who specialize in certain things, but they only pick up the scraps and have no actual power. But you were there last night. Something like this gets covered up, it blows up in everyone's faces. I hate cleaning up a mess. But I can't pretend my phone's out again, at least not this week."

"You want me to keep working the case."

"Learning *why* those three men died in there might not be important to the sheriff, but it is to me. There's interested parties who are no doubt happy they're gone. But there are others who will want Lucien Khar for what they believe he saw or knows. And the sheriff's willing to let him dangle in the breeze."

"What about Lucien's attorney?"

"Svetlana Petroff? Don't know her, except she's high end and worked for the family. Don't need to do much else if Shahid Khar's your client."

"I've got some people to talk to, then. Bonus if I can find who's after Lucien."

Barma nodded. "All right. If you need anything, call. Keep a low profile."

"You know me. My profile is my strongest suit."

Chapter Eleven

"You got Zoe involved in a shootout?" Dillan shouted.

Miles held his device away from his ear. *It was an accident. I didn't think what we were doing was dangerous.* Neither excuse would hold water, and any apology would sound lame.

"She's okay. She's safe and heading to work. Marshal Barma sent one of his deputies with her to make sure she makes it there."

Glenda had been uprooted from her desk with no small amount of grumbling. But once she was committed to stepping out into the heat of the day, she had donned a flak vest and helmet, both which looked two sizes too big, and had departed the station with Zoe.

Dillan said, "That doesn't make me feel any better. Are you expecting more trouble?"

"No. She sent me a message that she made it without incident," Miles added.

"She texted you? I haven't heard back from her in over thirty minutes!"

"Maybe because you were yelling when you talked to her when she was here."

Miles instantly regretted the words.

"Of course I was yelling. I got upset. And not with her, with you. Dad, you asked for a ride downtown, not for her to serve as an escort following the son of a ruthless criminal. You got her shot at and then had her driving at high speeds through Seraph like she was in an action serial."

"She told you she was driving fast?"

"I asked after I saw the car data service warnings. She earned us seven traffic citations."

"You're spying on her?"

"We rent that car. It's expensive. And we both pay the bill. Don't make this about me."

Miles took a breath. Reminded himself of something Seo Yeun could never drill into his head. At least if they were arguing, they were communicating. It was always better than silence if they could remain calm.

"Dillan, I'm sorry. Zoe offered to drive. I should have said no. I didn't think what happened would happen. I was trying to find a witness to a crime. I was going to hand it off to the marshal. Then, when I saw the witness get attacked, I stepped in. Zoe wasn't there, but she was waiting in her car."

His son's voice remained strained. "You're leaving out the part that this person of interest might have been involved in a murder. She texted me while she was waiting for you."

"It's true. Three people died last night, and the marshal needs my help."

"Is that why you wanted to come to Seraph? To join the marshal service? I thought you were retired."

"I am. I didn't come here for this. I came because you're here."

Silence. Then, "Dad, I have to go."

The connection ended. Miles stared at his device for a moment, almost called back, but put it away. Zoe's text informing her she was at work waited for him.

He replied, "I'm sorry about today. Are you all right?"

"Interesting morning," Zoe texted back. "I'm fine."

"Talked to Dillan. He's angry with me and I apologize for that."

"He was upset that I got cited for bad driving. Sounded more disturbed about the car."

It took a moment of writing and rewriting his response. "No, he's worried about you. Give him a break. I'm sorry I got you involved."

"Don't be sorry. Today was exciting. ☺."

"You working with people around you?"

"Plenty of people here at this hour. Should I be concerned?"

"No. I'm just being paranoid. But I want you to be safe. Have a good day at work."

He put the device away and caught his breath. Dillan was angry with him again, and Miles hated the sensation of his stomach twisting into knots. He'd have to talk to Dillan later. But for now, his son needed a cooling-down period, and he could only hope Dillan and Zoe wouldn't get into a fight over this.

But Lucien Khar was in the wind. As the only current witness, he needed to be protected, and Miles needed to learn what he had seen. The direct approached hadn't worked, even if it had been fortuitous in preventing Lucien's kidnapping.

Barma emerged from a room down the hall and sent a document to Miles' device. "Soil report from the shoes."

Miles read through the report. Silicon, calcium, oxygen, aluminum, magnesium, potassium, the list went on, labeling each by percentages. Insight tried its best to sort the data, but he stopped it.

"It's a match for the junkyard ground right outside the crime scene," Barma said.

"So he was there. Why don't you sound happy?"

"I took a sample of my own shoe for comparison. Inside of the container was rusty."

Miles scrolled to the bottom of the report. "You tracked more rust. And Lucien's shoes?"

"Didn't have much."

"Rust might have come from the other side of the container where you parked. Might be a patch of rusty ground where he didn't walk."

"Yeah. But without doing a thorough check of the ground and footprints, this is what I have for now. I don't think Lucien set foot in the container."

"So he didn't even see what happened. Whoever's after him probably doesn't know that. Can we tell Sheriff Vaca about the soil data?"

Barma dropped his gaze. "She hasn't changed her mind about this. I checked. We're out. I tried to call the Red District commander to see if we can share notes, but he just deferred to Vaca."

"What about the other interested parties? Xander Trowbridge's people. The Yellow Tigers."

"I've put inquiries out to find out who knows what. I'd say Vaca can't just cover over the murders, but anything's possible at this point. You could go ask questions."

"I detect a 'but' coming," Miles said.

"Yeah. Ask your questions. Gently. And you'd better leave my name out of it."

"As much as Lucien Khar is a dweeb, he's a priority if he's in danger."

"He has his bodyguards," Barma said. "But I agree. His bodyguards might not expect a genuine threat. You saw who was after him. What do you want to do?"

"Find him. And to do that, I think I need to talk to his lawyer. Can I borrow your car?"

Chapter Twelve

Unlike the marshal's station, Svetlana Petroff, attorney at law, didn't have a robot sentry with a burner facing down a visitor to her office. A pleasant young man in a white shirt and bolo tie behind the desk had Miles sit on a leather couch. Faint piano music played. Cool air descended from a vent. A crystal bowl held an assortment of wrapped hard candy. The wall art was drizzled lines of bright colors on rectangular blocks of black, weathered wood. Miles stared at the painting for a moment before deciding he hated it.

Svetlana came through a door by the reception desk. She wore a fixed smile devoid of warmth. "Miles Kim? You're from the marshal's office."

"Yes, although I'm not a sworn officer. Marshal Barma hired me to assist with his investigation."

"Come in, deputy."

She held the door open, and he entered. For a high-end attorney with a rarified criminal clientele, Svetlana Petroff kept things simple. A small desk, a couple of ferns, a wall screen monitor, and a floor-level window with lace sheers looking out at the ugly back lot.

The two red lacquered chairs had only a thin leather-covered cushion. Miles failed to get comfortable.

Svetlana rounded her desk and eased into a swivel chair, then turned off a tablet and folded it into its keyboard. On the desk was a hoop bracelet, rainbow colored, something a child might wear. She popped it into a drawer.

"Now that the marshal is no longer involved in the investigation, why are you here, Mr. Kim?"

"Your client Lucien's life is in danger. I need to know where he is."

"I think the marshal made the case for that earlier. Lucien has private security, quite capable. I vet them, and his father wouldn't allow me to hire anyone but the best. I appreciate you coming in person to remind us. Was there anything else?"

"You heard what happened to his father, your client, Shahid Khar?"

Her smile vanished. "Yes, I've been informed. News like this travels quickly. And considering my client, it made it to me with light speed. All of us here are devastated, naturally."

"And Lucien falls under your legal care?"

"Yes. I will continue to offer him counsel during this difficult time. In fact, I'm in the middle of a mountain of work. Do you have something you can add to what I know about the event that's relevant to your visit?"

Miles adjusted himself on the seat so his hip would hurt less. "I don't know what you know. I know Lucien was there."

"What proof?"

"Start with the car which he or someone in your office helpfully cleaned. His shoes. And we're only getting secondhand information about what else the Red Banners found at the crime scene."

"Is this an official or unofficial inquiry?"

"I'm not the marshal."

"And that's not an answer. Don't try to snow me. And whatever recording device you might be hiding in that noggin of yours, turn it off if you want to have a less formal conversation."

He made a show of tapping his head. "This old thing? My Insight module's so outdated, nothing it sees or hears could ever be admissible. But it's off. And like I said, I'm just assisting."

"Lucien didn't kill his father or the other two men," she said plainly.

"How can you be sure?"

"Because he told me. He didn't even know what happened inside that container except that there was a shootout and there was no one alive after. He looked in, saw his own father along with the other two men lying there, and he ran."

"Straight here?"

"What?"

"Did he come straight here, or did he stop somewhere first?"

Svetlana took a package from a drawer, shook a white mint into her hand, and popped it into her mouth. "He called me, then we met here. He was deeply distressed at what happened."

"He's an actor."

She crunched on the candy and chewed. "He's a boy who doesn't know what he wants from life, is on the six-year college plan with no degree, and he isn't capable of orchestrating this."

"I need to see him."

"Why do you believe his security detail isn't up to protecting him?"

He leaned forward to relieve the pressure on his hip, but the chair instantly began cutting circulation to his legs. "First concern is the people who came for Lucien. Pros. If his bodyguards aren't up to snuff, they're going to lose. Add to that, whatever went down last night has the sheriff and the Red Banners hiding a triple murder."

"You don't think he did it."

"I let the evidence talk. But my gut says no."

"And you trust me enough to share your speculations."

"Off the record, yes. Maybe it's because I don't know any better."

"Smart man, Mr. Kim. Perhaps if you've been up against me in court, you'd see me otherwise."

"My read is that you're interested in serving your client. It could be because without him and with his father gone, you're out of a job."

"Even with his death, Shahid Khar's business interests will provide me with enough comfortable work for the rest of my career. But I do care for Lucien. I saw him grow up. And his father was good to me, and I owe him. The question remains, can I trust you?"

Miles made a show of his hands as if he had nothing else to offer.

Svetlana sighed and worked her mouth with her tongue as if to dis-lodge something stuck in her teeth. "All right. I'll check with Lucien. Tell him you're coming. His bodyguards will have the final say if you get to stay. If they tell you to leave, you leave. If Lucien asks you to go, you go."

"Okay."

"One question before you get out of my office. Why did Marshal Barma hire you?"

"That's an easy one. Deep discount, and I came cheap."

Chapter Thirteen

"Get rid of him."

The bodyguard was a beefy thug with face inks which looked fresh and a bulging frontal lobe. His black and white checkered sports coat was stretched tight over his biceps and chest. The butt of a burner leaned out from a shoulder holster and didn't hide the fact it was a chrome plated monster of a weapon not meant for small spaces.

"We don't need him," the bodyguard continued. "He's going to get in the way."

A second guard grunted an agreement. He was leaning close to Miles, nose wrinkled, and looking him up and down like he was inspecting a piece of stinking meat. He wore a carefully groomed face of stubble, and his hair was slick and crispy with gel, which smelled of leather.

Lucien Khar had opera playing on a sound system. He sat in a lounge recliner with a stemmed glass holding a ruby liquor inside it garnished with a citrus peel. He wore oversized shorts, a brown silk shirt buttoned below his hairless chest, and a small hat and sunglasses.

They were on the back deck of Lucien's townhouse. Below them lay a willow-lined lazy river which ran the length of the exclusive complex, a landscaping feature which must have cost a fortune. Above the open-air courtyard stood vapor collectors like billowing sails. The air held moisture. A mother or nanny was minding a pair of children down below, who were wading ankle deep in the flowing water.

How everyone living in a Jupiter hab imagined life on Earth would be like after the return migration.

"You heard them," Lucien Khar said. "Get lost."

Miles gave Stubble Face a gentle but firm shove backward. "Not until I have my say."

"You had your say," Lucien said. "I have people after me. Hardly a new thing. I had two kidnapping attempts before I was seven. My complex has security. I have Theo and Matt to protect me. What else do you have to share?"

Stubble Face's grimace intensified. "Now you can leave."

Miles had lost track if he was Theo or Matt. "I only need a few minutes. You were at the scene. Did you set foot inside the container where your father and the others were meeting?"

Lucien sipped his beverage. Pointed to the air. "You hear that music? The Lonely Squire. One of the tin can operas which we hope to perform at the theater once we're done with Sartre. I heard a company in Pac City has a whole series of similar productions."

"You couldn't have missed the gunfire before you ran. Did you hear anything before or after? Voices? Parts of conversations?"

"We're going to place actors in set locations out of sight from each other, engineer acoustics to match what you might experience in one of the smaller habitats to recreate the experience of singing a duet or a trio with someone not in the same compartment. Imagine it."

"I'm sure it will be magical," Miles said dryly. "After the shooting, did you consider trying to see whether your father was hurt or needed help?"

"We would do the same thing with the musicians. A trumpet here, a clarinet there, viola and cello on opposite ends of the theater. The audience would be in the center of the experience, the stage nowhere and everywhere. Tell me, did your hab ever put on one of these productions?"

"I was five when we emigrated back to Earth. I'm sure there're archives."

Lucien waved off the suggestion. "Poor substitute for being there, and the recordings are terrible. I want first-hand memories to shepherd the project along."

"I'd rather talk about last night. We can discuss Earth and Jupe art movements another time."

"Perhaps I'm talking to the wrong Kim. Your son is involved in a stage production. Perhaps I should visit him."

Miles felt an icy grip on his heart. "What?"

"Your son Dillan. He's invested in the theater. A little financial push, and his fundraiser play could hit it big. Of course, I might have a few suggestions. And I never developed the taste for seeing young children on stage. Must be a parent thing. Untrained voices are one thing, but it's the reluctance I have no stomach for. At least they should wait until the child can grasp the material and develop a fire in their belly for the work. Why the long face?"

"My son has nothing to do with this. Or you."

"Of course he doesn't. I thought it prudent to know who was showing up here, implying I know or care what happened in the crotch-end of this sun-blasted hellhole of a town. If you have an accusation, tell it. Otherwise, I have no answers to your questions. There was a shooting. I departed. That is the simple answer."

"And I want to believe you," Miles said. "But there are others who won't take your word that you know nothing. I get it that you got scared and left. From what I saw, there wasn't anything you could have done to save your father."

"Save him?" Lucien spat. "Save him? I wouldn't save him if he were burning alive before me and I had a bucket of piss to douse it all out. Scared? Of course, I was scared. I didn't want to be out in that garbage pit in the middle of the night. When the burners started firing, I jumped in the car and left. When he didn't call, I knew he was dead."

"Where did you drive to right after?"

Again, the hand wave, as if the conversation could be fanned in another direction. "It doesn't matter. I'm tired. I'm tired of you and this conversation."

Stubble Face took Miles by the arm and walked him through the townhouse towards the exit. The music got louder. The door slammed behind him. But even through the door, Miles could hear the melody.

He knew The Lonely Squire. While he didn't have his Insight module until he was grown and a soldier fighting in the war, the songs of the opera had been firmly etched in his young mind. He had never understood the words. The singers had sung it in its original Korean, and his parents had stuck to English at home. Two singers plied their voices. Separate, but joined in song. A haunting sadness to the refrain, a love lost and never to be united. A longing for a life they could never have.

That, at least, was the story his five-year-old mind conjured, even as he later learned the tale in the opera wasn't anything remotely romantic, the eponymous squire merely reminding his lady that her horse was prepped for the day's ride.

He preferred his own interpretation.

The duet followed him out to the street.

Voices together in space, yet separated by a void, forever alone.

Chapter Fourteen

The two people who were watching the front of Lucien Khar's building hadn't moved from the shady spot beneath the ash tree since Miles had returned to the marshal's parked car.

He had taken the first spot available, which was in the sun. Barma's vehicle's interior broiled. The seat and steering wheel were almost too hot to touch. A selection of food wrappers lent the driver's compartment an aroma of spoiled meat and rancid dipping sauces. But for the moment, he endured it all as he watched the car with its two passengers. Zooming in, he saw one man, one woman, both neat grooming, but not expensive neat. Likewise the car. A plain sedan trying to be too plain.

Cops.

Without the decals, there was no way to know who they belonged to. Red District, Yellow Tiger, Sheriff Department, or some fourth-party security firm. But besides their superior parking spot, they didn't appear to have noticed him.

Who they were might be less important than why they were there.

He got out of the subcompact.

One cop, the woman, perked up as he approached the back of the vehicle. She was fighting with her seatbelt as he crouched next to her door and knocked on the window before showing his hands empty.

"Got a sec?"

She rolled down the window. An older officer, working out of uniform, patterned blouse and cricket cap, with a snub-nose slug thrower in a shoulder holster. "What do you want, Mr. Kim?"

"I guess introductions aren't necessary. Can I see some ID?"

The driver leaned forward. Older man with a bulbous nose which had been broken more than once in the distant past. "You can see the tip of my boot when it gets planted up your ass."

The woman gestured for the man to stop. Pulled a Yellow Tiger ID card with her identity and a badge. Detective Louanne Ringer.

"What are you doing here, Mr. Kim?" she asked.

"Concern for my fellow citizen. And I wanted to know who else was visiting. You guys security detail, or here to question Lucien? Red District militia has the case, doesn't it?"

"We're here to keep the peace. Your presence isn't necessary."

"Good that everyone here is of the same mind in that regard. Since we're both off the investigation, maybe we can share notes."

The driver scoffed. "Share notes? Louanne, get rid of this guy."

"There's nothing to share," Detective Ringer said. "Lucien Khar is a person of interest in a major crime, and we're here to make sure Red District doesn't drop the ball. We're still lead law enforcement in Seraph, so I'm going to ask you to vacate the area and don't come back."

Miles grin was one-hundred percent professional curtesy. "Since you asked so nicely. Before I leave you to it, do you have any idea why the president of your agency was meeting alone with Shahid Khar and Xander Trowbridge?"

"Leave."

It had been worth a try. Sometimes a rank-and-file detective might ache to share something they knew. He'd have to check with Santabutra Sin and see if the detectives were who they claimed to be. He didn't want to use his connection with her for this, but he was out of fresh ideas.

As he headed for the car, he hurried to get out of the way as a cruiser bearing Red District markings sped in his direction. A pair of cops got out. Miles was ready to raise his hands, expecting a pat down and arrest, but the officers ignored him. They were moving down the sidewalk, heading straight for Lucien Khar's front door. The Yellow Tiger detectives got out of their vehicle and moved to intercept. The four militia cops began talking loudly and pushing at each other.

"You have no operational authority here!" Detective Ringer shouted at one of the Red District troopers. "Get back in your car!"

"We have a warrant to detain the witness," one of the Red District men yelled back. "Orders of the Sheriff and our commander. Don't like it? Call your supervisor. Now get out of our way."

Both the driver and the second Red Banner trooper appeared ready to pull their sidearms. Miles put a parked utility van between him and the four officers.

Something barreled down the sidewalk towards him. He dove aside into the space between the van and Barma's subcompact.

A robot delivery dog, that was all. A delivery dog doing its thing. But on the sidewalk? Something was wrong.

The silver robot sprinted smoothly past, almost soundlessly, and raced straight for the four officers.

"Look out!" Miles shouted.

But the officers weren't paying attention.

The dog wasn't stopping.

And when it got close, it detonated.

Chapter Fifteen

Smoke, a rain of dust, and a ringing in Miles' ears.

He spat as he tried to keep his balance just to sit up. The explosion had shifted the van sideways. It now rested in the street ninety degrees to the sidewalk. The front half was peeled open as if it were a rind of a metallic fruit. If there had been anyone inside, they were gone, along with the engine. The other vehicles closer to the point of detonation were likewise torn to shreds. A shallow crater stood where the officers were, and there were no bodies, no delivery dog, nothing.

He stood, but the world swam and he fell. Tried to touch his face, clear his eyes, check himself for injuries. He worked his jaw, but the ringing threatened to overwhelm him.

Shapes moved in the swirl. Phantoms or zephyrs. But he saw feet. Insight identified combat boots, make and model, but failed to uplink with Seraph net to check for nearby vendors.

The boots came, the boots left, more than one set. Somewhere distant, another explosion. Burner fire. He reached for a weapon that wasn't there.

The Caretaker spiders came at night, but sometimes would attack in the middle of the day just to change things up.

And when the boots ran past a second time, Miles felt the world slip by.
***

"Give him another," a female voice said.

A second woman standing close replied, "Wait a moment, Captain. He's coming to. Be patient."

"This is taking too long."

Sheets. Miles felt smooth sheets. Nearby machines hummed, and distant voices echoed from a hallway. He lay in a bed in a white room. Attached to either arm were monitors and a hydration line. Oxygen cannula fixed to his nose. An itching sensation began at the tip of his metal fingertips and ran up past the elbow to his shoulder and along his neck and into his head. But his movement was restricted, his left arm encumbered by the cords and his artificial right arm refusing to move at all.

He fought back a wave of panic. It was like being paralyzed.

"Hello, Miles. I'm Imani, your nurse. Can you speak?"

"Barely. Where am I?"

"Wood Creek Hospital. Do you remember what happened?"

He tried to nod and regretted it instantly as he fought down a wave of nausea. "A bomb."

Captain Sin leaned in to get a look at his face. "I need to speak with Miles privately."

"He needs to rest."

"He will, after he talks to me."

The nurse departed and closed the door as she left. Santabutra's expression softened. "How are you feeling?"

"Like a nuke went off next to me."

"Early guess tells us it was a mining charge strapped to the bottom of a delivery dog. Express service says the unit was offline, so someone hacked it."

"There ought to be a law."

"You could have been killed. What were you doing at Lucien Khar's house, anyway?"

Miles fought to prop himself up on an elbow. "What happened to the cops outside?"

Santabutra shook her head. "We lost them. Two Yellow Tiger detectives, both twenty-year vets. Red District officers both had families."

"What about Lucien Khar?"

She took a moment before replying. "Missing. His bodyguards were shot up. One's in a coma, the other didn't survive the ambulance ride."

Miles let the news settle in. "There was a team there on the tail of that dog."

"And we're investigating. Lie back and rest. It's not your business. Marshal Barma is in the loop, but it's out of his hands, too. Sheriff's orders."

"And Yellow Tigers do what the sheriff says?"

"It's how things work here. The mayor directs the sheriff. The sheriff assigns cases not part of our organization's mandate."

"Save the fine print. Who's going to find the kid?"

"Red District has investigation authority. This is big and ugly enough that my militia is helping with checking for witnesses and electronic footage, anything which might show us who the perps were and where they went after."

Miles studied her for a moment. "Your agencies are working together all of a sudden?"

"It's complicated. There's unpleasant history, but if everyone keeps their head and does their job, we might get something done."

"From the look on your face, you haven't found anything."

"I'm not part of it. I'm still on admin restriction pending the internal probe follow-up after the Agatha Fish matter."

"You told me not to ask you about that," Miles said. "How's it going?"

"This is why I don't date cops."

"Ex-cop. And officially we aren't dating. Has Red District shared anything about the shooting at the junkyard?"

She cut loose with an irritable sigh. "I'll tell you because what I know isn't through official channels. But they wrapped the investigation up by noon today and reported it as a double murder. Shahid Khar shot Trowbridge and Patton and was likewise gunned down. Neat and clean."

"Except no one knows why they were there in the first place without their guards."

"What does it matter?"

"It matters for Lucien Khar. He was there, and someone believes he knows something."

Dillan stuck his head in the door before entering. "Hey." He kissed Santabutra on the cheek.

She rose and patted Miles' leg. "Get rest. Dillan, call me if he tries to leave before the doctor says he's cleared."

Miles watched her go. He found he had enough strength to fiddle with his unresponsive cybernetic arm.

"What's wrong?" Dillan asked. "Let me get the nurse."

"No nurse. It's my arm. They unplugged it."

"Dad, there're bandages."

"If the connection is intact, I'm reconnecting it."

Dillan assisted, and the limb was back in operating condition after a moment of fussing. He clenched and unclenched his hand as the virtual sensations returned. He unplugged the PICC line feeding him the saline and removed the oxygen tube on his nose.

"Stop it," Dillan said.

"Look, I'm grateful you're here. But I'm not spending the day inside this place. I want to go back to my hotel. I'll get rest there."

"You haven't even told me what happened. No one has."

"There was a bomb. Someone killed four cops and kidnapped Shahid Khar's son. That's the case I was working on. I'm off it now. Like I told you, I'm sorry about bringing Zoe along with me earlier. But the bad guys took what they wanted. And all I want is to get out of this place, go to my hotel room, and lie down in my bed."

Chapter Sixteen

Miles climbed out of the car at the curb in front of his hotel. He fought to keep steady, not wanting Dillan to see how wobbly he was.

"Let me at least walk you up and get you settled," Dillan said.

Miles raised a bag of supplies they had picked up from the drug store. Bandages, rubbing alcohol, body wipes, groceries. "I've got what I need. You have your event. You only checked your phone eight times while we were in the store."

"I'll call you this evening. You're going up and straight to bed?"

"I promise."

He went to the hotel entrance and watched as Dillan drove off. Was about to march back out when a fresh wave of dizziness hit him. He gripped the door to keep from falling.

Maybe an hour's rest. It was late afternoon, just after four. A nap, and then he could decide what to do and how to proceed. He caught his reflection in the door. His clothes were a mess, and his hat had a tear, leaving part of the brim dangling. At least his device had survived the blast. Turned it on.

No messages.

He'd have to check in with Barma. If Red District handled the abduction like they had the scene of the shootout, they'd scan it, clear it, and forget it.

If Barma could get him access to any surveillance footage from the explosion, Miles hoped he could start his own search. Insight hadn't seen enough to have a clear picture of the event.

The clock was ticking. Every moment the perps had Lucien was time they might extract whatever they wanted to learn from him. They needed him alive only long enough to share what he knew, even though Miles couldn't shake the gut feeling the kid knew nothing.

Kid.

Not a kid. A young man living an extended childhood. Playing up how dangerous he was by dangling the fact he knew about Dillan. So did he sit out of the fatal meeting where his father had met his end because he wasn't interested, or had he not been invited? Surely Lucien was smart enough to know that his father wouldn't meet with the likes of Xander Trowbridge and Bing Patton unless it was important and profitable.

Too many dangling questions. His head hurt.

Miles almost cried out in surprise when the dog came running at him from across the street. It jammed its muzzle against his side and started whining. Miles stroked its head and side and gave it a pat.

"I missed you too, buddy. But I need to go in there, and you can't come."

Did Seraph have an animal shelter? Only then did he realize Insight hadn't rebooted. He left the mental switch alone. Promised himself he'd check for a shelter first thing. After his nap. The dog's whine grew especially pitiful when Miles stepped into the lobby.

The manager was asleep at his desk behind the partition.

Miles made a kissing sound, and the dog hurried to his side. They climbed the stairs together.

***

An hour later, he lay on his back, feeding chunks of a wrapped date crunch bar to the dog, who sat attentively on the floor with its snout on the sheets. It had drunk its fill of water and then some, and had been perfectly quiet so far.

The ringing in his ears was an unpleasant buzz which felt like it would be around for a while. Dillan had purchased some painkillers along with the other supplies. Miles had taken none. Wouldn't. Felt exhausted, but his mind kept churning.

If what he had seen from the Red Banners and Yellow Tigers was the best they could do, Lucien Khar didn't stand a chance. And Marshal Barma appeared more concerned with toeing the political line than solving last night's murders. It was all spiraling.

Not my business, he reminded himself. *Not anymore.*

But the questions kept coming. Who would be brazen enough to blow up a group of militia? What could Lucien possibly know to be worth taking that kind of risk?

He texted Marshal Barma. "Any surveillance footage you can link?"

After a minute, Barma replied. "You're supposed to be convalescing. Heard you left the hospital."

"I don't do hospitals. The footage?"

"We're done. My office has no access to the investigation. Thanks for the help."

"Talk?" Miles typed.

"No. Finishing supper, and then I'm going to sleep for a week and hope Tigers and Banners don't shoot each other to bits while I'm out. Here's your stipend for today."

A credit link pinged on his device. Hardly a fortune, but it would pay the rent for the next few days. Instant, no restrictions on how it could be spent. So unlike a Meridian paycheck, where the credits had to be used on limited things and couldn't be saved, as they would expire. No wonder so many had struck out to settle in Seraph and places beyond.

Miles texted, "Hear any word on the victims' devices? Messages sent before the meetup? Financial transactions? Someone preparing to pay for something?"

"It's the sheriff's business now."

That was it. Barma was quitting. Sleeping for a week sounded like a good idea. But Miles couldn't. The dog had curled up and was snoring when he climbed out of bed. Sunset outside. The hotel was getting loud as his neighbors on either side were just getting in, talking, and turning on their serials at high volume. The dog had no problem snoozing through it all.

He turned on Insight. Two hours until his overnight security shift began at the construction site, assuming he still had a job. But there was no notice from his boss to indicate otherwise. Minor miracles.

To Tristan he texted, "Come get me before work?"

"Can't. Will barely make it on time as it is."

With limited bus options, Miles knew he'd have to walk. Calling Zoe or Dillan was out of the question. But then he checked his balance. With the stipend, he had enough for a rental, and a quick check on Seraph net confirmed a service could send a vehicle over. Expensive, and after a week he'd have to give the car up and he'd be back in the same position of needing to scrape for rides.

He clicked his tongue. The dog looked up, immediately alert.

Miles said, "What do you say we go out and find us a ride of our own?"

Chapter Seventeen

The electric motorbike was more of a scooter with a long rear rack meant for strapping cargo. Plus it was used, the engine difficult to start, and eggshell blue. But it ran, and the dealer let him off the lot with a few credits to spare after withstanding a withering round of attempted upsells.

He had just under an hour before his shift began. The dog balanced on the back, leaning forward and occasionally bumping against Miles during hard turns. But Miles kept his speed down, uncertain of how hard he could push the vehicle. Plus, as his head was still ringing, he was worried about his own ability to navigate the Seraph streets without killing himself.

"We have a discount on helmets," the salesperson had offered just before Miles had departed, said without a hint of irony.

The Bright Blocks neighborhood lived up to its name in the early evening, with hundreds of lights of every imaginable color shining from the container homes. The streets between were barely lit, though, and Miles had to concentrate lest he plow directly into one of dozens of steel walls jutting into the roadway. But soon enough, the ground grew rough, and he left the lights behind as he crossed the berm into the vast junkyard west of the city.

Without Insight as his navigation aid, he doubted he would have found the exact location of the crime scene. Another reason to believe all three victims had their devices, plus any type of map program in their cars. They had met at the prearranged spot at a precise time. He doubted any of them were excessively familiar with the area.

He slowed the bike as he got close. He scanned each narrow lane in search of any other vehicle. Surely Red District had secured such a sensitive site, but for the moment he was alone. Perhaps the militia had scoured it, cleaned the crime scene, and left. He parked at the mouth of the alley. It was empty. Both of the other victims' vehicles were gone.

"Stay," he told the dog. It whined once before sniffing about the mud where Miles had parked his bike.

He didn't know what he was expecting to find. Nothing, he felt certain. Not his circus, not his monkeys. *Closure*, he thought cynically. One last look, and he could excuse himself and go back to his night job and let the sheriff sort out the mess.

Yellow DO NOT ENTER tape crisscrossed the middle of the alley. Miles ducked beneath it and pulled more of the tape away from the door leading into the container. He clicked on his flashlight and shined the white beam about. Took careful steps forward as he approached where the bodies had lain.

The table and chairs had been pushed against the wall. Blood still marked the floor and furnishings. At least the dead had been removed, but the rest appeared as it had been. Whatever analysis had taken place must have been quick, using scanning software and photography.

Miles detected no scent of forensic chemicals, further leading him to the conclusion that this was a rushed investigation. Scuff marks of a dozen boots had obliterated whatever story the blood spatters on the floor might tell.

He crouched for a few minutes next to where the table had stood and tried to imagine the event.

Three shooters unloading in rapid succession. Three deaths. Besides streaks in the grime, the floor told him nothing new. A single burner hole in the ceiling. Final shot as one victim fell. Burner blasts rarely penetrated a human body and came out the other side. The hand-sized weapons didn't pack enough punch.

He walked a careful circle, trying to imagine the chairs where they had fallen. But he had seen enough to know no one else had been sitting there, and there was no sign Lucien Khar had been at the table. And unless the young man had come in barefoot or in socks, his shoes hadn't touched the floor of the cargo containers.

What were the facts? Three bodies. They had shot each other, judging by the location of the wounds. Bing Patton had blasted Xander Trowbridge with the shotgun. Shahid Khar had the chrome pocket burner, a better fashion accoutrement than a defensive weapon. Miles didn't know if he had gotten a shot off. But the third weapon, the military-grade burner, had been emptied.

Trowbridge's gun. And laser wounds had taken down both Shahid and Bing. Without the bodies, there was no way to know how many holes each man had in him.

More facts. Besides Lucien, the three had met alone, and they had known when and where to meet. The Red Banner militia now held the vehicles and personal possessions that might shed light on any communication between the victims and other parties prior to the shootout.

And finally, all three victims were powerful men, wealthy, with major pull in Seraph.

Next came suspicions.

Red Banners and Sheriff Vaca had an interest in keeping this all to themselves.

Miles checked the time. If he wanted to make the start of his shift, he needed to leave. Yet he remained crouched. Trowbridge had cut loose with all twelve shots. Some had struck Bing and Shahid, but not all.

One burn hole in the ceiling that he knew of. He played the light around and saw no more. He leaned over the table. Two more neat, melted perforations, both penetrating the plastic. He walked a wider circle, still trying to avoid the blood. Another round had hit the corner of the container near the rear curtain. And then three more in the wall. From the table to there, it was reasonable that Trowbridge's frantic burst had been the source. More misses than hits, but enough had found their marks.

Miles froze.

Next to the rightmost burn hole was a smudge. Grease? Mud? He shined the light and leaned close, almost putting his cheek to the metal.

Blood. A blood mark with a fourth burn inside it.

Bing had fired his shotgun in the opposite direction. And a burner wouldn't carry tissue like this. Laser wounds cauterized, and there was little spray. This was too big. Someone had been standing here and had caught a burner round and had been close enough to fall back against the wall. Perhaps they had been leaning. Perhaps many things, but Miles stopped himself.

What were the facts?

There had been a fourth person present, everyone investigating had missed it, and whoever it was had made it out of the container alive.

Chapter Eighteen

Miles felt his hands shaking as he took out his device.

He wanted to call Marshal Barma. This was his department. But Barma had made it clear they were no longer involved, and Miles didn't think an appeal of any kind would get Barma off his rear and back into the investigation, a potential witness and possible new suspect be damned.

Calling the sheriff would get him arrested.

That left Santabutra. But whatever she might bring to the table, it might put her in a compromising position, aiding an interested party with no legal reason for trespassing on a crime scene.

He put the phone away. Through the curtain, he inspected the area in search of anything he might have missed. The back entrance yielded nothing. The floor was grimy, dirty, and covered with mud and boot prints too muddled to recognize with a quick examination using a flashlight. Outside was the second alley where he and the marshal had first met. More gravel and oily mud. No telltale blood trail.

A Meridian crime scene drone could sniff out blood and all the trace elements. So could a trained dog, operative word "trained." He went back inside, moving inch by inch, checking walls and ceiling, but he had missed nothing. He played the light beam back across a panel of wall and its adjoining portion of floor.

Did it look cleaner than everything else?

It was just off the main track where passersby would walk if they were cutting through the containers, so there were no boot prints. But it also lacked the grime. He crouched and slid a finger along the ground. Clean.

It took a moment, but the steel wall had a discernable seam. The precise cut allowed no room to pry easily, and Miles didn't have a knife or tool. He pushed. The panel didn't budge.

Checking outside, the outer shell of the shipping container was too high to climb without a boost. He went back in and through the curtains to the crime scene. The plastic chairs had nothing which would help. But he flipped the table to its side. The edge was metal. With his right hand, he bent a section back and forth, back and forth, until it snapped. Smoothed an edge. This he brought back to the secret panel and worked it.

The panel leaned and he pulled it away, breaking part of a plastic lip which was holding it in place.

A tunnel led into darkness. The striated steel walls and low ceiling were part of the surrounding containers. Crawling was the only way. While Miles wasn't particularly claustrophobic, the thought of being trapped in the narrow space gave him pause. Another smudge of an old blood stain up ahead caught his eye. He went forward.

The clean patch gave way to a film of gunk, alternately slick and sticky. A reek of old oil and heady fumes penetrated his sinuses. His throat started burning and his chest grew tight. He blinked tears away. The hard metal beneath him did his knees no favors as he did his best to hurry.

Dead end.

The steel wall before him felt smooth and didn't budge. He tried his impromptu pry bar, but there was nothing to latch onto and he only bent it. The light showed no seams. Yet somehow, someone had come this way. He cocked his right arm, preparing to punch the wall, but stopped himself. Breathed. Ignored the pinching in his lungs. His head felt loopy. Crawling back was the only way to go, but at the moment he feared he might pass out, and if he went down inside the crawlspace, he feared he wouldn't wake up.

He reappraised the steel surrounding him. Had missed nothing. He fumbled with the flashlight for a moment. Dropped it. Was it his imagination, or did he detect a faint cool puff of air? He switched the light off. A dim glow came from a line in the wall just behind him. He shoved. It didn't give. But a square in the section of wall was cut out. He backed up for better leverage, braced his back against the opposite side of the corridor, and pressed every direction he could. The panel slid to the left, haltingly at first, and then it fell away and clattered loudly, the *ka-rang* echoing about the enclosed space beyond.

A lamp burned orange in a small room. The air smelled different, but still held a distinct chemical odor. Disinfectants, bleach, something, along with a putrid smell, human, with a hint of sewage and unwashed bodies.

Someone was sprawled on a lumpy bedroll in a shadowy recess. Soiled bandages lay strewn about. Wrappers of medical supplies likewise had been dropped or cast aside, along with cut clothing and containers of medicine.

Miles fought to stand, his joints complaining with a drum riff of racks and pops. He stifled a cough.

Whoever was on the bedroll wheezed.

"Hello? I don't want to surprise you. I'm Miles Kim. I'm not a cop. I'm not here to hurt you."

He did his best to appear harmless and show he wasn't armed. He edged closer. It was a young woman lying before him. Gauze covered much of her head, neck, and one arm. A saline drip bag was hoisted on a crude bent wire fixed to a wall. A box next to her overflowed with more soiled wrappings. The stench grew stronger. Blood and pus soaked through her dressings.

He brushed black hair from her face, but much of her head was recently shaved. One eye was completely bandaged and wept a yellowish ooze. Crude, seeping stitch work ran across one side of her jawline. Her left shoulder was wrapped. The wound appeared to be about the right height for the burner mark back at the container. On one arm, a burner wound, not new, a pucker mark along with old stitch marks, perhaps a month old.

A hand with purple fingernails reached for him. Her one eye flashed with recognition. "Miles?"

He took her hand. He knew her. The woman who had pretended to be the Herron-Cauley lawyer on his train ride to Seraph. She was the bounty hunter who had let him go in favor of stealing the item that had triggered the Seraph Express robbery. She had also suffered a burner wound on her arm.

"Dawn Moriti, what are you doing here?"

Chapter Nineteen

"What happened to you?"

Dawn's eyes fluttered. "Get...me out of here."

Miles made a careful examination of her wounds. The bandages on her head, neck, and arm were more than what would be needed for a single laser burn. Someone had performed wholesale surgery.

"I don't know if it's safe to move you."

She squeezed his wrist. "Hurry. Before they come back."

"Who? Who did this? You were in the shipping container during the shootout. You got hit."

"Yeah, genius, I got shot," she said through clenched teeth. "And then someone found me and did this. They tore out my implants."

He had too many questions. But if someone was going to return to continue their work, he had no weapon. She feebly grasped for the line in her arm but was too weak.

"If I get you up, it'll hurt you, maybe kill you."

"If they catch us, we're both dead."

He pulled the cover off her. Her legs were undamaged. He gently detached the saline drip. She was shivering. He wrapped the sheet around her and lifted her.

"Why...aren't you packing?" she asked.

"I'll explain later. Do you have a vehicle?"

"Don't know. They took everything. Can't imagine they left it."

A single door led outside. When Miles pushed it, it shuddered. Something was holding it closed. He delivered a solid kick. Something broke, and whatever latch had been set fell apart. He nudged the door all the way open with his back and got them out. They emerged between large containers partially submerged into the ground. Above was the night sky, the stars obscured by haze.

Miles was turned around, and Insight was having a moment with its compass. The alley between any of the containers was tight enough that carrying Dawn would prove difficult. He was about to choose a direction when he heard a dog bark.

Dawn's breathing came in ragged gasps.

"Hang on," he said.

He changed course and hoped the passageway would get him close to where he had left his bike. He didn't want to shout for the dog in case there really was someone nearby. The thought of what had been done to her sent a chill down his spine. And he pushed aside the dizzying notion she was involved in the violence from the previous night. Her presence meant her life was in danger once word got out.

The dog appeared at the mouth of the alley. Its eyes reflected the meager light and it chuffed as Miles inched along, mindful of not bumping Dawn's head against the metal.

They were on a wide lane which led to the alley. Miles' bike waited for them.

"You're going to have to hang on," he said.

But Dawn's head lolled. She had gone completely limp.

From somewhere behind them came the wrapping clang of metal on metal. The signal was answered by someone closer by, a softer *thud-thud-thud,* steel on plastic. A shrill hoot rose from the dark, which caused the dog to bark.

"Shut up," Miles hissed.

With Dawn clutched in his arms, he straddled the scooter seat and fumbled for the controls. Hit the starter switch. Nothing. He slammed the button and gritted his teeth as the engine popped, puttered, died.

Motion in front of him. Someone had just run across the wide lane which led deeper into the junkyard.

A sharp hammering followed by a hoot. Another voice answered with an identical cry. They were close, too close.

"Come on, machine."

Miles pressed the button deliberately and firmly and didn't let go until the engine clicked, whirred, and hummed to life.

He began the awkward process of scooting the bike into a sharp U-turn.

"Dog?"

He wasn't sure what he would do if the animal ignored him. But it sprang up onto the back of the scooter and nearly unbalanced them. He planted a foot to avoid spilling over, reasserted his grip on Dawn, and grabbed the handlebars.

Something whizzed past. Insight tracked it as the bottle shattered against the side of a shipping container.

Miles squeezed the accelerator and the bike lurched forward. They wobbled precariously, hitting a rut as the tires fought to find purchase on the slick sand.

Someone jumped in front of them. Miles gunned it and they struck the figure, sending them tumbling aside. Miles kicked down to stop them from falling, got the bike rolling forward again, and gave it everything it had.

Gravel sprayed. But he kept them upright, willing the machine to not die, to not stall, and to get them out of there alive.

Chapter Twenty

"Where are you going?"

Dawn fought to get each word out. She clung to consciousness and threatened to drop out of his arm if his attention lapsed. They were navigating Bright Blocks. Insight kept wanting them to turn down the smallest streets, but Miles doggedly ignored it, intent on using the route he had used to get them there.

He kept squeezing the accelerator. "Hospital."

"No. Anywhere but there."

"You're dying. They ripped your implants out."

"Yeah. Was there for that. But if you take me to the hospital, they'll kill me."

"Who? Those butchers?"

She tried unsuccessfully to shake her head. "No. Meridian."

"Then where?"

He couldn't hear her response. When he chanced a look, he saw she had passed out again.

How many junkies, battered spouses, and bleeding criminals had tried to refuse medical care, as if their prospects would be worse if they ended up in the hospital? But with Dawn Moriti, all bets were off. Someone was willing to kill Seraph cops to get at what she knew or had witnessed. So what did all three victims have to do with Meridian? While the corporation governed River City and its surrounding territory, their boundary ended halfway to Seraph. That didn't mean Meridian's reach stopped there. Everyone suspected they had agents in Seraph and Pacific City. But it was mutual business concerns which kept the peace between the three governments, along with a common hatred for the Caretakers.

The thought that Meridian agents might be behind the violence was a level of complication beyond his understanding.

First things first. He had a dying woman who needed care.

If the hospital was out, then where? The hotel was no good, and Barma wasn't reliable enough to trust with this. The sheriff and either militia were both suspect. And while Dillan might have a medical doctor in his contact list, he couldn't bring this kind of storm down on his son.

"Call Santabutra Sin."

Insight complied, and his phone rang.

"Your girlfriend?" Dawn muttered.

"Not my girlfriend, just a friend."

"She's Yellow Tiger. You can't..."

"Right now, we don't have a choice. I'm driving, and it's my call. She's the best bet for getting you someplace safe."

Dawn tried to reply but her face tightened as she winced. "Mistake," she managed.

Santabutra answered. "Miles? You understand I sleep nights."

"It's important. I have someone who needs a doctor, a clinic. Someone discreet, and not the hospital."

"Why not the hospital?"

"I can't explain right now," he said.

"Does this have anything to do with Lucien Khar and the shooting?"

"Don't ask me that unless you really want to know."

A long sigh. Santabutra said, "I'm trusting you to know what you're doing. But my trust has limits."

"I wouldn't call you if I had other options."

"That makes me feel special."

Miles came to an intersection and adjusted his load. The dog nudged him. "I need a place to go. I'll tell you everything once I get there. If you can't, I understand. But you have to choose now."

"Keep it together, Kim. I'm looking it up. Sending you the address. But I'm warning you. This better not get me in deeper with my bosses. I'm up to my neck already, and I hate the smell."

The address pinged, and Insight suggested a rather swoopy route to get there.

Miles got them rolling.

Before hanging up, he said, "I'll keep you out of this. I promise."

***

Much like the Yellow Tiger militia station, the trauma center had imposing walls around it and a gate. Spotlights clicked on as he pulled up to a call box with a staring eye of white light. Before he could say anything, the light twinkled and the gate rolled open.

A team of three in green hospital garb waited for them, a gurney in place, and they took the unconscious Dawn from his arms and laid her out on the gurney before raising it and wheeling her through a set of automatic doors. Miles parked his vehicle next to a row of ambulances and first response motorbikes. No Yellow Tiger insignia. Each vehicle featured the letters A.L.T. in an oval, streaking left to right in a circle with a tail, like a comet. The A.L.T. insignia was on the doors as well, which swung open for Miles as he entered the clinic.

Cold blue lights illuminated a tiny empty waiting area walled off with glass. One of a pair of receptionists looked up from her work.

Her eyes narrowed. "No dogs."

"Oh, him?" Miles asked. "He's with me."

"Saying 'He's with me' doesn't make it okay. We can't have dogs in the trauma center."

Miles plopped down on one of the hard chairs and put out his hand. The dog wedged itself next to him and he patted it. "If anyone else comes in and complains, I'll take him outside."

The receptionists muttered between themselves, but Miles ignored it. Took a moment to catch his breath. On the wall behind the receptionists were a pair of black carbines. He hadn't seen armed medical since the war. What kind of trouble did they expect at a private hospital?

He knew he should look up A.L.T. to see what kind of facility this was and who it serviced, but he was too tired and had a pretty good guess. This was a private hospital where anyone who could pay for the extra security would go. Whether it was militia or just for the wealthy, he had no idea. But Santabutra had pre-cleared them, and Dawn was getting the care she needed.

The dog nudged him when a doctor in scrubs, AR glasses, and a facemask emerged. "You brought in the patient?"

"I'm Miles Kim. How is she?"

"Being prepped for surgery. We don't have any information about her. Who can we contact for medical records?"

"No one. She's new in town."

"You must know something. We're running a check on her bio signatures, but nothing's coming up."

As Miles expected. Dawn had wiped his records clean, so he could only imagine she was a ghost, if she wanted to be.

"At least tell us her name," the doctor said.

Captain Sin entered the waiting room from the parking lot. "N.N. will do, Doctor Pham."

Doctor Pham blinked, and his glasses shifted colors. "Please inform the receptionists if you decide you can share anything. 'Nomen Nescio' has had her implants forcibly removed, has been shot, and has unknown drugs in her system that will take us time to sort out before we can sedate her."

"Do your best, doctor." She waited for him to go before sitting down next to Miles. "Start talking."

"This is impressive. Yellow Tigers hold a contract with them?"

"Yes. Red District, too. There's this place for serious injuries, and two clinics, plus they send their doctors out when needed. Not just us. Mining and construction companies, people like Herron-Cauley, anyone who wants extra security and discretion. But that's not what I want to talk about."

"She was there at the shootout," Miles said. "Front row seat. Caught a burner wound."

"Who is she?"

"I'm sure I don't really know, but I can guess. Dawn Moriti, if that's even her name, is an opportunist. She's got skills and had high-end implants and probably worked for the upper echelons of Meridian. Intelligence service, I'd wager. She came after me. But then she cut me loose when the opportunity presented itself to take what the Metal Heads stole off the Seraph Express."

"Which was what?"

"Three people died trying to buy it or take it from her. The people who snatched Lucien want her and what she has."

Santabutra scowled. "And now she's here. Just great. I can't just make this go away. A visit here generates paperwork."

"We saved her life. Between you and me, we can figure out how to proceed."

"You're not supposed to be involved. This is you handing off a mess, whether or not you believe you're helping."

"No one has to know she's here," Miles said. "The doc admitted her anonymously, didn't he? N.N.? That's your code for a John or Jane Doe?"

"Yeah, but people aren't stupid. Both militias have access to all the hospitals' databases. I don't know who Dawn is, but I know where you found her. You triggered a crime scene alarm. Red Banners sent a patrol out, and they're combing the scene right now. Tell me what they're going to find."

Miles only needed a moment to think about what he had discovered. The blood stain. The secret panel. The passageway to the room where he had found Dawn.

"I didn't have time to tidy up," he said.

"So I guessed. Whatever happened to Dawn Moriti is horrific. You did a solid by saving her, Kim. But right now she's in just as much danger as if you had taken her to Wood Creek Hospital."

"You were my only option. I don't know any underground sawbones. She was dying."

"Yeah, all right. What's done is done. Now I just need to figure out what happens next. I'm going to get some of my people here quietly, because this place isn't made to do more than discourage anyone who might cause a problem." She put on her monocle. "And Kim? Who brings a dog into a hospital, anyway?"

Chapter Twenty-One

Yellow Tiger militia showed up right before sunrise.

Dr. Pham had come out for an update an hour before and informed Miles and Santabutra that the patient had been stabilized and was going to survive, but there would be complications. Whoever had ripped Dawn Moriti's cybernetics out from her had shot her up with a cocktail of drugs to keep her from thrashing during the involuntary procedure, and they had been less than careful.

"They didn't get to her medulla implant, thank god," Dr. Pham said.

Miles tried to force the fog out of his head. "Maybe that would have been round two. She was hooked up to a drip bag, so they were caring for her to some extent."

"Perhaps. N.N. is not out of the woods yet. I'll keep you posted."

Now, with two additional cops inside, the waiting room felt cramped. One consulted with Captain Sin in a hushed, urgent conversation. When another pair of officers arrived, Miles took the dog and stepped out for a breath of fresh air.

Paramedics were preparing one of the ambulances, loading it with supplies. A chill clung to the air even as the light reflected down off a neighboring building.

He had ignored messages from Tristan.

"Where are you?" "You're making me handle the shift alone?" "Past midnight. You there?" "So bored!" "I'm doing your rounds for you." "You dead? Hope you're dead because I'm handling everything right now." "Sorry about last, please reply." "Clocking us out. You owe me big time."

Miles was about to reply when a militia tank rolled up to the gate. Also Yellow Tiger. But the group that deployed out of the vehicle carried rifles, were armored, and they appeared ready for business. The paramedics stopped their work and stared as the group waited to be let in.

Santabutra marched out of the clinic and towards the gate.

Miles recognized the officer in charge of the newly arrived group. Lieutenant Chindi. But he was wearing captain's bars on the collar of his chest piece. Someone had received a promotion since their last encounter.

Chindi stabbed the call box button and peered through the bars of the gate. "Captain Chindi, Yellow Tigers. We've been assigned security for the clinic. Let us in."

Santabutra turned a key in the manual lock override. Now the receptionists couldn't buzz the gate open remotely.

"Captain Sin, what are you doing?" Chindi asked.

"Sealing the clinic, Captain Chindi. We already have a security detail here."

"And you're not in charge of it. You're on administrative leave. Open up now!"

Santabutra gave Miles a weary look before returning her attention to their new visitors. "I'm a sworn officer of the Yellow Tigers, and I'm authorized to act in harmony with Seraph law when confronted with an emergency like this."

"Like what? Nothing's been filed, and you've commandeered active militia units outside of proper channels."

"I don't report to you. Just because you're out of the loop doesn't mean I'm violating civil or corporate regulations. This situation is under my control. Who called you here?"

Chindi didn't answer, instead talking on the radio to his squad.

Santabutra stepped closer to Miles. "I can only hold them off for so long. They'll have backup soon."

"Someone at the clinic must have notified him," Miles said. He pulled out his device.

"What are you doing?"

"Making a call of my own. What's the average militia response time in this part of town?"

The Red Banner cruiser pulled up behind the Yellow Tiger tank. A second unit followed, parking across the street, and soon a third.

"What did you do?" Santabutra whispered.

"Now it's a party."

"It's a Red Banner investigation. If you're really trying to keep your friend out of their hands, you failed."

"Your Tigers were about to swarm in. I had to do something."

The two militia groups were arguing. Captain Chindi waded into the confrontation, but was met head-on by a Red Banner officer who wasn't backing down. Hands were on holstered weapons. The voices got loud.

Santabutra joined Miles as they retreated from the gate. "What did you tell them?"

"I requested Red Banner send a unit here to stop a group of rogue Yellow Tigers or someone impersonating them from stealing medical supplies."

"This is no good. They'll sort it out soon enough. I'm sorry, there's no way we can keep your friend safe. Red District won't be as polite as the Yellow Tigers. Where are you going?"

Miles headed into the clinic. Using Insight, he mapped the place out as best he could as he charged past the reception desk and through the door labeled No Visitors and Trauma Team Staff Only. The dog was on his heels, but Santabutra stayed behind at the entrance. He spotted two other exits, clearly marked by signs. But none of it would mean anything if Dawn Moriti couldn't travel.

A doctor or nurse in a gown intercepted him. "You can't be back here."

"I need to lay eyes on my friend who we brought. Which room?"

She got in his way and raised a hand to stop him. "Sir, please go back to the waiting area and I'll get the doctor."

"I don't need him. It's urgent."

She looked over her shoulder. For a moment Miles thought she was about to lead him to Dawn's room but instead she raised a microphone on a com device she was wearing around her head.

"I need security—hey!"

Miles took the device and flung it into a hazardous waste bin before brushing past her. She was shouting now, and the trauma center wasn't that large. He only had seconds. The heart of the facility centered on a large nurse's station, and clear glass separated the patient recovery rooms, each visible. Miles saw one man in a bed connected to machines. Otherwise, the recovery rooms were empty. Scratch that. One had its curtains closed. He moved straight past another nurse who didn't stop him.

When he entered through the curtain, Dawn was pulling on a white pajama top. She had fresh bandages on her head, arms, and body.

She kept placing a hand on the bed to steady herself. "How could you bring me here?"

"You were dying."

"And now I'm leaving. Don't try to stop me."

He grabbed a pair of slippers from an open cabinet and placed them on the floor before her. "I'm not. You're in trouble. Both militias are here. I didn't have the chance to explain much earlier to you, but they both want you."

"That's why this place is a mistake. I'm burned."

He helped steady her as she slid her feet into the slippers. She tried to walk past him but had to pause and almost collapsed in the doorway. The nurse from earlier was storming their direction with a cop following right behind.

"All right, Miles," Dawn said. "Get me out of here, and I'll make it worth your while."

"That's him," the nurse said, as if there was a lineup of trespassing cyborgs to choose from.

The security guard was all hands and tried to move Miles along while grabbing him. "You were asked to step outside. Come with me."

Miles shoved. The guard stumbled and fell. The nurse screamed. Miles took Dawn and guided her towards the nearest exit. She was leaning by the time they made it out into an alley between the trauma center and the outer wall. Large air units hummed away, and a dumpster sat before a secondary gate that had electronic locks.

An alarm began bleating.

Miles had to hope the militia was still squabbling, because it would only take a moment for anyone to catch them once a search started.

Dawn led them to the dumpster. "Boost me up."

"This is no good. You're ready to collapse."

"Do it or I go alone."

She didn't weigh much. It took barely any effort to get her on top of the dumpster. She didn't wait, grabbing the wall, swinging her legs over, and slipping down on the opposite side.

The dog barked.

Miles climbed to the top of the wall. "Sorry, buddy. You're on your own."

The shouting from the front had only gotten louder, but the alarm drowned out everything else. Miles dropped to the sidewalk on the opposite side of the wall. Dawn rushed ahead, out of place in her white robes and looking exactly like an escaped patient. She peered around the corner.

"I'll get the bike," Miles said.

She clenched her jaw like she wanted to say something, then nodded.

Miles jog-walked past the militia clustered around the trauma center's main gate. One of the Red Banner cops pushed a Yellow Tiger. The Tiger responded by pulling his weapon. More shouts, orders from each to "Stand down" and "Back off."

He brought the scooter around to the alley.

Dawn hobbled over and grabbed hold. "Go!"

Miles took his device out and texted. "Just a sec. There. All right, hang on."

Her grip was tight on him as they sped off.

"Who did you message?" Dawn asked.

"Keep your shirt on. I needed to make sure someone would take care of my dog."

Chapter Twenty-Two

"This is my safe house."

He had to help her up the two steps to her small home. It was one in a line of similar cottages, with tiny front yards lush with flowers, vines, and miniature trees. Decorative fences ran around each property. An old man was pulling weeds from the neighboring sidewalk. He nodded at them as Miles tried the door. It was a mechanical lock with no thumb or keypad for entry.

She pointed at a flowerpot with a red bromeliad. "Under that."

A key waited beneath the plant. He took it and let them in before giving the watching neighbor a wave. The neighbor only stared.

Miles closed the door and set the bolt. "You have a hidden key for your safe house?"

"And nosy neighbors. If someone wants to break into something, they break in. That's always been one of my specialties. The only way I stay truly safe is by being anonymous. You should move your scooter. There's community parking at the end of the lane."

Miles made a quick check of the interior. Single bedroom, bathroom, galley kitchen, and a living room with a sliding door to a rear yard about the size of a wide parking space. "Not what I expected for you."

She had made it to the kitchen and was rummaging in a cabinet. "What *did* you expect?"

"I guess I have no idea. But the way you left me after the train, I imagined your place being a high-tech tower with surveillance, disguise kits, robot underlings, and racks of weapons on the wall."

"That's in the basement."

She brought out a package of tea. But from it she produced a needle along with a wrapped bundle of ampules. Miles watched as she prepared a shot and injected it into her belly.

"What's that for?"

"Counter the sedatives they gave. I'm ready to collapse."

"You were in surgery only hours ago. You should be in a hospital. At least lie down and rest."

"No time."

She pulled a ventilation grate from the wall and slid out a small duffel bag. Inside were weapons and gear.

"Now what?" Miles asked. "Planning on going on the run with a brace of burners while wearing a bathrobe?"

"I lost something important the night before. I need to look for it."

"Sit down. You're about to keel over. Start with telling me what happened."

"Look, thanks for getting me here. I owe you. But I'm not prepared to answer questions, and knowing you, you're going to keep asking."

"You're not the only one in trouble. The people who are after you took someone. Lucien Khar."

She blinked hard a few times, then winced. "Lucien. Lucien Khar. Shahid's son? What does he have to do with this?"

"Problem with your implant?"

"Yeah. They were sizing it up to tear it from my skull. The surgeon sewing me together didn't do me any favors. Tell me about Lucien."

Miles filled a teapot and clicked it on. In moments, the water was churning inside. "He was there last night. Word got out."

She nodded gravely. "How long ago did they take him?"

"Yesterday afternoon."

She sat. Waved vaguely towards one cabinet. "Tea and cups are there. Pour me one. All I have is instant."

"What happened out at Bright Blocks?"

"If they came for Lucien, you're on the list too, just for knowing what I'm about to tell you."

He set down two cups and filled them with hot water. Each received a dollop of desiccated powder. "Three victims, not counting you. Four interested parties. Two militias and the sheriff involved in figuring this out. Start anywhere, I'm all ears."

She snapped on one burner and checked its charge before setting it down. "You have people you care about in Seraph."

"The fact you haven't kicked me out or shot me means you need my help. I need to know how to save Lucien Khar."

"It might be too late for him."

"I'm not giving up before I start. If I had, you wouldn't be here."

"There's a radio device I had for sale. Old tech. Not worth much to anyone, unless you know what to do with it."

"An old radio? The three dead men showed up to buy an old radio?"

"Yeah. It's a shuttle transponder. Caretaker tech. None survived the war, at least as far as anyone stuck on Earth is concerned. It might mean a way to see if anyone up there is still watching and listening. Maybe it's a way to open communications. That's it. That's the gadget, and that's what someone wanted from the Seraph Express. I put the word out it was for sale. Trowbridge, Khar, and Bing Patton agreed to meet my price."

"Big enough purse for them to need to coordinate their effort?"

She gritted her teeth as she rode out a wave of pain. "Big enough so I can vanish and never have to deal with things like this ever again."

"Does this have something to do with the explosion in River City? News said it was the Caretakers dropping a rod from up high."

"That might have been an accident. I can't say. But there are Meridian agents looking to retake what I stole. The three idiots who I thought were coming together to buy it off me sounded smart enough that they wanted to work together on how to best use it. You saw what happened."

"Yeah," Miles said. "They shot each other to pieces. Shot you too. I'm still not tracking how a transponder would be worth the trouble."

"Seems the later generations have lost their sense of imagination and have gotten used to life on the ground. I guess they got the idea from somewhere."

The implied accusation hung heavy. "When the war ended, there wasn't much choice. Nowhere to go with all the junk flying above us."

"A lot of that junk has fallen," Dawn said. "We can go back up there if we try."

"You're sounding just like a Meridian executive. But you're the one who wants to sell out and go retire."

"I never said retire."

She was sweating now. She loaded another ampule into the injector.

Miles placed a hand on hers. "Wait. I don't know what you're thinking, but you can't go back out there. You can barely stand. Stims won't stop your body from shutting down."

"You sound like you care."

"I don't understand what this shuttle radio of yours means. But whoever has it took Lucien. I'll look for it. Give me a chance to do that before you run off and die trying."

"This isn't stumbling around the desert searching for a rogue machine head. Meridian agents are no joke. They're deadly." She set the injector down, unused. With her one eye completely wrapped, she was hard to read. "I'm going to get dressed and go out to the junkyard. Someone has my transponder. I need to get it back before it gets stripped for chips and jumper pins. If you want to help, then help."

But as she tried to rise, she pitched forward, tilting the table and sending her teacup tumbling. Miles caught her.

"Let go," she said.

"How were you planning on finding it? Stumble around the west side wastes hoping to bump into the perp who did this to you?"

She didn't have an answer. Was incoherent as he took her to the bedroom and got her to lie down. He squeezed her hand until she focused on him.

"I'll take care of this," Miles said. "You coming isn't an option. From the sound of it, no one knows you're here. Stay put and I'll check on you later. So if there's anything—anything—you can tell me which will help, tell me now. For starters, what does this thing even look like?"

But Dawn Moriti had fallen asleep.

Chapter Twenty-Three

"They're looking for you. Kim, are you listening?"

Miles' scooter engine had come up short as he tried to pass a double trailer big rig on the boulevard. He had a large sedan behind him, honking its horn. And the truck next to him had sped up. Miles couldn't squeeze the accelerator any harder. Finally he waved an apology and let the truck overtake him, but was then almost run into the opposite lane as the sedan passed on his right. The driver signaled her displeasure with a single upturned finger.

"Kim, can you hear me?" Santabutra asked. "Are you there?"

"Yeah. Morning traffic."

"Where are you?"

"Trying to survive on Seraph's fine roads. Who's looking for me?"

"The trauma center has footage of you taking their patient away. So safe to say, both militias want you to find out who she is. That's the official line. But Sheriff Vaca seems to have put two and two together, and she's putting the screws to me to share what I know."

"You know nothing. Tell her that."

"Thanks a lot. Tell me why I'm putting my pension on the line for you."

"Because of my winning smile."

"You're harboring a key witness to an investigation. They've got you assaulting a security guard. And they know I provided access to the trauma center to you. If your friend was there last night and you have her with you, that puts you in company with the most wanted person in Seraph. So cut the arrogant tone."

He made a turn and found an open lane. "Neither of us wants to see Lucien Khar hurt. This is my best way forward. I can't share more than that, because right now I don't even know if what I'm doing will help. But I know the sheriff isn't going to get this done. And after what I learned, there's more to this than we understand."

"Not new news. I can't help you anymore."

"Is that why you're calling?"

She hesitated before answering. "I called to tell you one last time to be careful."

Navigating the junkyard in daytime was oddly disorienting. Between the shipping containers and trash were heaps of scrap, some appearing deliberately sorted and shaped, or his mind was playing tricks on him. But every so often an impaled stuffed toy or a steel-frame scarecrow leaned askew from the rubbish. Scraps of rotten clothing clung to stakes like guidons. Husks of burned or melted vehicles were stacked along one lane near the scene of the shootout.

No sign of the denizens who had chased him that night.

Five minutes after crossing the berm into the scrapyard, he spotted his first patrol. A Red Banner tank stood parked at a crossroads. None of the troopers were visible outside or in the turret.

He made a sharp U-turn, but couldn't quite come about and had to push the scooter with his legs a few paces back before he could head in the opposite direction.

Classic blunder, he chided himself. Evasion was cause enough for them to stop a potential person of interest. But the buttoned-up tank made no response as he sped off. They'd have cameras and advanced sensors, along with drones, if they were being aggressive in their search. He could only hope they weren't paying attention.

He took a circuitous route to where he had found Dawn. No cops around, at least not yet. He parked by a leaning chain fence topped with razor wire that marked off a lot occupied by a colossal disassembler and a material handler with a giant claw large enough to snatch up a bus. A hand to his holster confirmed the burner he had borrowed from Dawn's collection was in place.

Having it on him felt like he was committing to a course which might take him beyond anything which could be overlooked by a responsible officer of the law, be they Santabutra Sin or Marshal Barma. But the thought of encountering whoever had performed surgery on Dawn made him realize it wouldn't be a polite encounter.

Keeping in the shadows, he moved to the mouth of the container and strained his ears. No voices. The inside of the makeshift operating room remained as he had found it: the blood-stained bedroll which had served as the surgical table, the strewn bandages, the dangling saline bag.

But not all was the same. Someone had switched off a lamp that he had found burning.

Dawn had mentioned "they" would come back when he had rescued her. And so they had, no doubt to finish what they had started. No reason to believe it wasn't the same people banging the pipes and throwing bottles.

He checked the entrance to the crawlway through which he had discovered the impromptu surgery room. It remained closed, and he only saw his own footsteps in the grime. So the Red Banners and whoever else was after Dawn hadn't discovered it. As their search broadened, he couldn't count on them missing it for much longer.

Boot prints marked the ground around the bedroll. Too many to track easily, but Miles got the sense it was three people. So who had found a cyborg in the middle of a trash jungle and arranged for her disassembly? Brutal, but they hadn't killed her. And did they have any idea what the transponder was?

This was no alleyway snatching by cyborg hunters. This felt like a target of opportunity. But the saline and the drugs, those wouldn't be something someone just had on them.

Echoing voices carried from somewhere beyond the container. Metal squealed. Muffled radios. The heavy tromp of boots on steel, and Miles knew the militia were inside a nearby container. Whatever measures Dawn had taken to wipe all traces of her passing might not keep them from finding this spot.

Time to leave.

But as Miles stepped outside, he saw in the doorway a partially dry yet glistening glob. Spit? He crouched to inspect it. Reddish brown. Betel berry. Nasty habit found among the earthborn, which had spread through Meridian and points beyond since the homecoming.

He returned to his scooter. He flinched when the disassembler on the opposite side of the chain fence started up, the croaky motor sputtering and sending up a plume of dark smoke. A vibration rolled through the air that rattled Miles' teeth.

He went around to a rolling gate that had a chain and lock hanging open. When he moved the gate aside and stepped onto the lot, someone shouted.

"Hey, get out of here!"

Miles gave a friendly wave. "Hello?"

A heavyset man wearing a leather hat and dirty blue apron approached, flanked by a second man with a crowbar.

"I said get lost," the man in the apron said. "Private property."

Miles spoke up to be heard over the machine. "I couldn't help but notice your equipment and was hoping to ask a few questions."

"No questions. Go, or get thrown out."

"Fine. All right, I'm going. I was looking to buy clean scrap. I'm a motivated buyer with credits."

"Not selling any scrap," the man in the apron said. "That's your business, take it elsewhere."

His colleague twirled the crowbar.

It would be too easy for these to be the people who had attacked Dawn. They didn't appear interested in him or his implants.

"Thanks for your time," Miles said.

"Now get." To punctuate the order, he spat a wad of brown juice onto the dirt.

Miles turned as if to leave. "Say, you wouldn't happen to know a good surgeon?"

The two men exchanged a look. Then they spread out and flanked him.

Miles raised his hands as if to placate them. "No need for things to get out of control. I'm not a cop."

"Didn't take you for one."

"Militia is right around the corner looking for some bad guys. What this is so far is a friendly conversation."

The man sneered. "They won't hear anything over all this racket. They've been by already. And you're asking dangerous questions."

Miles placed his hand on his holster. "What I am is armed."

"Oh, that little thing." Mr. Apron grinned and reached behind him, revealing a gold-plated firearm. Seven shot, high caliber, iridium sights, and a name in ruby cursive on the barrel too swirly to make out.

Insight had both men targeted. Miles' hand did the rest. In one motion, he had his burner drawn, aimed, and powered up with a satisfying hum all before Mr. Apron could untangle his weapon from the drawstrings of his clothing.

"This *little thing* is twitchy," Miles said. "You have two choices. Put that pimp gun back in your pants where you found it, or I take it away from you."

Crowbar was licking his lips as if on the fence about whether to attack or run.

Mr. Apron said, "Old models like you don't normally move that fast."

"I had my shots this morning. Put the gun away."

Two heartbeats later, Crowbar went for it. Miles rotated, fired, pivoted, and fired again. Both men fell to the ground. Crowbar was moaning and clutching his abdomen, while Mr. Apron had a hand clamped to his wrist. The gold pistol was at his feet. The name on the barrel read "Robby." Miles took it and flung it into a scrap bin next to the disassembler.

"You shot me," Mr. Apron said.

Miles holstered the burner and crouched. "Yeah. Tell me what happened in that container."

Mr. Apron clenched his teeth and glared. Miles leaned in and went through his pockets and took out a device and a pocketbook with a picture ID and credit chips. Also a packet of ground betel nut.

"I...I need a hospital," Crowbar said.

"What is this?" Mr. Apron asked. "A robbery?"

Miles inspected the ID. The man's name wasn't Robbie. "Right now, it's a conversation. Tell me what happened."

"We didn't do anything."

"You didn't rip the implants out of a woman for salvage? You were in there. If I search your yard, what will I find? If I have to go rummaging and turn up medical supplies and cybernetic microtools, this gets a lot less friendly."

"It wasn't us. It was...there's a mechanic who knows about this stuff. Name's Brookie, and after we found her unconscious, I called him. That's it!"

"You were in there. I saw your spit, genius, and your boot prints are everywhere. It's only a matter of time before the Red Banners drop by again. Did you miss the fact they're turning over all of Seraph looking for her?"

"She was alive," he said lamely.

"Barely. Now tell me what happened."

"I found her unconscious and bandaged up. But she had all that hardware, so I called Brookie. She had high-quality parts, and he knows what to do with them."

"And?"

"He came and set up shop and did his thing. That's it. It wasn't anything personal. She looked like she was on her way out. No one comes to this part of town if they have anyplace to go or anyone looking out for them. How were we supposed to know?"

"Yet here we are. Does Brookie know his victim is gone?"

"I told him the Red Banners were snooping around and figured they found her."

"And if they didn't? Was he planning on coming back to finish his work?"

Mr. Apron hesitated to answer. Finally, he nodded.

"I'm really hurting," Crowbar mewled.

Miles considered the device he had taken. Locked screen. "Where can I find Brookie?"

"I only have a number. No address."

"Open your device and show me."

Mr. Apron's hand shook as he thumbed the phone and unlocked it. Brookie was one of the first contacts. No address. And Miles felt with certainty the surgeon wouldn't answer if someone he didn't know made contact.

"Call him."

"What do you want me to say?"

"Tell him besides finishing what he started, you have an old cyborg that could use some attention."

Chapter Twenty-Four

Miles paced as he waited. For good measure, he kept a target square on the scrapyard operators. Both men sat up against the tracks of the material handler. Miles had found a medical kit and allowed them to treat their wounds and take something for the pain.

Probably better care than they had given Dawn Moriti.

A long motorcycle with balloon tires pulled up by the scrapyard gate.

"That's Brookie," Mr. Apron said.

Miles gestured for Mr. Apron to join him. The man winced as he rose, either putting on a show or the painkillers hadn't completely numbed his arm.

Good.

They walked towards the gate. The motorcycle rider stepped off his bike. He wore a head wrap and goggles and was tall and thin. He checked a wrist device and looked around as if searching for something. Then he caught sight of Miles.

"What is this?" Brookie asked. "There's militia here."

He appeared ready to get back on his bike. Miles nudged Mr. Apron.

"We have business that's worth it," Mr. Apron said. "I wanted to introduce you to our new friend here."

"No, dog, this isn't right. Calling me in the middle of the morning? This place crawling? I'm gone."

"Wait," Miles said. "The cops were by, but they left. My friend here says you can hook me up with what I need. Let's take this conversation off the street."

"This fossil is our new client? And what happened to your arm, dog? No, this is no good."

Brookie backed up and clicked on the power to his bike.

Miles tried to approximate the shakes of someone suffering through withdrawals. "I've got credits."

"You also have a gun. It's making me anxious. And he's hurt. Feels like I'm interrupting something."

Mr. Apron kept quiet and was watching them both nervously.

"Just an accident that could have been much worse," Miles said.

Brookie turned off the bike again. "I don't like it." He got close and appraised Miles, giving him a once over and looking closely at his cybernetic arm and face. "Upgrades aren't cheap."

"Like I said, I have funds."

"On you?"

"I'll load up a chip with enough to settle the bill, if the price is right. But I want to see your inventory."

"I don't know. You're old, dog. Prosthetics don't always take well if you have any issues with your immune system. You tripping or detoxing? That makes my work more difficult. How are your bones?"

"Good, last time I checked."

"Then hand over the burner and we can talk."

"Out in the open like this?"

"I'm not setting foot in that salvage yard, if that's what you want. I trust these boys less than I trust a prospective customer I've never met with zero references. I have a tablet here with my inventory. Hands, arms, eyes, can even replace a hip while I have you under. Could even do a bundle discount, assuming you have the credits."

Miles pulled the burner free and removed the battery before handing it over. Brookie took it and set it on the bike seat without comment. The surgeon's arms were covered to the wrist, and he also wore gloves. Besides his nose and mouth, he had no skin visible. He took a tablet out from a saddlebag. By a remote, no doubt an implant, the screen winked on and soon Miles had a scrolling selection of cybernetic parts.

"No prices listed," Miles said.

"All I'm showing you are pictures, dog. Once I get an idea of what you want and you show me you have the juice to pull the trigger, we talk turkey."

"I don't want anything you've had sitting in some junkyard warehouse for years. Just the air out here is corrosive. Sort by recent acquisitions."

Brookie gave an exaggerated nod. "All right, all right. Don't appreciate the implications and the impugning of my catalog, but the customer gets what the customer wants. Tell me about what you're wearing there, friend."

"Meridian surplus. Hoping for something which won't ache when the weather gets cold."

The tablet resorted the display. While Miles didn't see an acquisition date, the implants were newer, with many late models his Insight module didn't recognize.

"There's new, but then there's compatibility," Brookie said. "From what I see you wearing, it won't be a simple swap and plug kind of deal." He gave Mr. Apron a look. If their MO was to jump a victim, Brookie wasn't getting the signal he needed. Or maybe the surgeon wanted the credits first.

Miles made a show of studying the scrolling catalog. "You have some nice stuff. Before I fill my shopping cart, tell me what you have in the way of radio equipment. Something like what you'd see in an old airplane or space shuttle. Like a transponder."

Brookie looked confused. "Not what I carry and not what I do. What is this? Dog, if your bird here isn't serious, then we're wasting my time."

"I'm as serious as a heart attack. The woman you waylaid and operated on had one in her possession. I want it back."

"What are you talking about?"

"I saw what you did to her. She's alive, no thanks to you, and you tore her eye and hand apart. And I'm guessing you were planning on taking what she had in her head out next."

The wrist blade snapped out from beneath Brookie's hand and slashed at Miles. Miles blocked the blow with his metal arm. Brookie pushed and was too strong and soon the weapon was heading for Miles' throat. Miles kicked. His foot landed solid and punted the tall man backward. He fell against his bike.

Miles grabbed the burner and snapped the battery in. But before he could power his weapon up, a pair of Red Banner militia appeared. They were aiming rifles at Miles.

"Weapon down! Weapon down!"

Miles raised his hands and then, slowly as possible, placed the burner at his feet.

The two troopers kept their rifles on Miles as they came closer. Both wore armor with visors down. They'd call for reinforcements in moments.

So close.

Miles licked his lips but knew there was nothing he could say that would help. They'd arrest him and charge him with the ever-increasing list of offenses he had been accumulating since accepting Marshal Barma's offer to investigate the shooting. They'd question the surgeon, but if they didn't know who he was, he'd be in the wind with the transponder.

Lucien Khar's chances of survival were slipping away.

But before Miles could speak, a pair of palm-sized pistols snapped into Brookie's hands from unseen devices up his sleeves. He unloaded. The four sharp *cracks* exploded from the weapons, blasting holes in the plastic armor and sending both troopers to the ground. Miles rolled aside, getting the bike between himself and Brookie.

Brookie sprang to his feet and mounted the motorcycle, revving the engine before peeling away, kicking up a spray of sand.

Miles snatched up his weapon and went to his own scooter. The surgeon was out of sight by the time he got his engine started. Miles raced in the same direction, leaning forward and gripping the accelerator and willing the tiny engine to give it everything it had lest his quarry slip away.

Chapter Twenty-Five

Miles was heading towards town again. The junkyard avenue that held the cloud of dust from the fleeing motorcycle was a straight shot, crossing the berm and leading into Bright Blocks. But that was where a half-dozen routes opened, wending through the stacked cargo containers in every direction.

Had he lost him?

He paused, his electric scooter growing silent. While the big bike he was after might be loud, Miles' ears rang from the gunfire and still buzzed from the explosion outside Lucien Khar's home. At this rate, he'd be deaf by the end of the week, assuming he survived.

While much of Bright Blocks was a junkyard, unlike the refuse-strewn wasteland to the west, it was populated. Makeshift homes and apartment blocks on every street, some with vehicles outside. People were about, walking and riding everything from bicycles to desert runners. While the traffic wasn't heavy, it felt like the neighborhood was awake and had its share of people on their way to work or whatever occupied their day.

Miles picked a direction, leaving the wide-lane avenue in favor of a surface street which passed between triple-stacked blocks of red, blue, and green.

He paused by a group of children. They were dressed in vibrant colors, but simply. Shirts, skirts, pants, sneakers, mostly clean, but some not, and much of the clothes appeared ill-fitting and some with holes. The boys had closely shaven heads and looked uniformly lean. Girls wore ribbons or barrettes in their hair, and a few had colorful plastic bracelets.

"See a big motorcycle pass this way?"

They stared at him wide-eyed. He drove on.

More kids were about as he approached an intersection. A stout older woman in a high-visibility vest held a red flag in his way and stopped him as the children moved into the street.

"Where's everyone going?" he asked.

She made a face as if the question was beneath her. "Where do you think? It's a school day."

Miles felt his cheeks grow hot. Even in the squalor, there was school, and it was the middle of the week.

"Did a big bike come this way?"

The crossing guard waved the last of a large group past her. Her smile was bright, and she greeted a few of the kids by name. Once they were past, the smile vanished. "What are you looking for?"

"A motorcycle. Someone driving fast."

"No one like that here—good morning, Danielle. April. Ginny." Three more kids shuffled past. The red flag went down.

Miles was about to go. The neighborhood alone would take all day to drive through, and any of the thousands of structures might hide the surgeon, or none of them. He had lost his best lead. Going back to shake down the two scrapyard workers was no good. The militia would be swarming the place by now.

The crossing guard returned to her station and watched the last of the children vanish into an open gate marked with a sign. Crestway General School. Without looking at him, she said, "No, sir, no bike speeding through *my* neighborhood. Driving like a gentleman, on the other hand..."

The street beyond the school led to a market square. Shoppers crowded the stalls where baked goods, produce, flowers, and crafty knick-knacks competed for business. The lane was packed enough that Miles, along with a few other vehicles, could only inch along. But the market appeared to be inside a massive courtyard. The only way anyone could drive out was the way Miles had entered. He found a place to park near a van where a worker was unpacking clothing and placing them on a rolling hanger. He gave Miles a dirty look.

"Be back in five," Miles said.

Past the van lay a parking lot. At the far end waited the motorcycle. A vendor passed him with armloads of small cages holding pigeons. Other people moved about the lot, but none of them were the surgeon.

While the market had only one drivable street, small alleyways were everywhere.

Miles inspected the spot where the bike stood parked.

Reserved, a painted strip on the concrete read. But for who? He searched for a sign, a QR code, anything which might indicate who operated the lot. He then followed the wall of a container to where a cut door stood. He knocked.

The little girl who opened the door couldn't be older than three. Miles heard the muffled sounds of melodramatic dialogue playing somewhere behind her and beyond stacks of clutter.

"Is your mom or dad home?"

She nodded. Didn't move.

"Can you please get one of them?"

She vanished and a moment later, an elderly man with two canes appeared. He murmured under his breath as he reached the door and tried to close it.

Miles put his foot in the way. "Just a sec. I'm looking to rent a parking space for my company. Who do I talk to?"

"Me," the man said with a creaky voice. "None available. Move that boot or lose it."

"Everyone who rents pays you?"

"Aren't you a bright one?" He pushed the door, but Miles kept his foot in place.

"One of your clients rides a big bike. Brookie. Maybe I can double up with him when he's out. I'm happy to go ask."

The man made a sour face. "Do whatever you have to do. You're making me miss my stories."

"Which place is his, and I'll get out of your hair."

"Brookie? You mean Dr. Brook? Where else? Try the hospital."

Of course, Bright Blocks had a hospital.

The wide steel doors led to an interior waiting room with plaster walls, a glass barrier, and chairs, along with a play area for children and a muted wall screen showing a cartoon with a fairy and talking mushrooms.

A sign at the entrance read "Please Approach an Open Terminal."

The waiting screens stood on stands. Each had a woman's face on it. As Miles stepped up to one, the screen said in a neutral voice, "Please state the reason for your visit. Do you have a medical emergency?"

An A.I., Insight identified.

"I'm here to see Dr. Brook. I don't have an appointment, but it's an emergency."

"What is the nature of your emergency?"

"Biomechanical implant failure."

"Please scan a fingerprint and tell me as much about yourself as you can. If you have a medical record with us or linked through Seraph net, we will complete the virtual form."

Miles abandoned the sign-in screen and went straight to the window where a flesh-and-blood receptionist waited.

She glanced at Miles. "Finish signing in, please."

"I'm here to see Dr. Brook."

"What time is your appointment?"

Miles stepped aside as a mother and child exited through a door in the glass. "It's right now."

"Dr. Brook isn't seeing patients until this afternoon—hey!"

Miles caught the door before it could close. He walked past hospital staff and patients, glancing in each room. The receptionist was up and after him. "You have to stay in the waiting area! Come back here!"

Every door was open, with some empty and others with a patient waiting or staff member cleaning. At the end of a hallway, he found a close door and opened it.

A wide-eyed Dr. Brook spun when Miles entered. He was standing by a counter and unwrapping his arms, in the process of removing the two quick-draw rigs replete with levers and springs. His brace of pocket pistols sat before him.

"What are you doing here?" Dr. Brook asked.

The receptionist came charging up behind Miles. "Doctor Brook? I couldn't get him to leave."

"It's okay, I'll talk to him."

Once she left, Miles closed the door, not taking his eyes off the doctor. Neither of the doctor's weapons appeared ready to fire.

"You shot two cops back there," Miles said.

"I did what I had to do, dog. They'll live." He removed the rigs and placed them in a cabinet drawer before moving around a makeshift desk.

Miles took his burner out. "How about you stay standing where I can see you?"

"There's no need for this. I don't know how you found me so fast. The scrappers don't know who I am, do they?"

"Couldn't say. Let's talk about Dawn Moriti."

"Who?"

"The victim who you cut the cybernetics from."

"I assure you, she felt no pain."

Miles examined his burner. Both men he had shot at the scrapyard had only suffered minor wounds. But this model had a selector switch which ramped up the intensity of the laser at the cost of using more of the charge. He clicked it from one to three and the weapon responded with a faint whine.

The doctor's face had a mask of dust where the goggles hadn't shielded him. He had his eyes on the burner. He pushed hair from his face. His voice quavered.

"The high-end eye piece and hand I took from her will keep this place running for a month."

Keeping the gun trained, Miles began going through cabinets.

"What are you looking for? Drugs?"

Miles slammed a cabinet and opened another.

"I can get you Lift, pure Shabu with nothing that will make you go blind, Barbs, Nummers, anything."

The next cabinets held little more than gloves, glassware, and general medical supplies.

"What can I help you with?" Brook pleaded.

"You sold her implants already?"

Dr. Brook offered a wan smile. "I take them straight to my dealer, not here. He paid me already. There's no knowing where her parts are now. What, did you think I'd have them stored here in a crate?"

"I'd watch your tone right about now. During the war, there were smart guys like you around who knew the conflict would end and that there was a way to make bank off the pain. They printed armor plates on the cheap and swapped them out with the good inserts, using that for grist for whatever they wanted to print. They stole drugs. Ever see someone with head-to-toe burns scream because the anesthetics the medics used were nothing more than a flavoring agent with some scent added to fool the doctors?"

"This is nothing like that. I don't know your friend. A Seraph dilettante who wandered into Bright Blocks in search of a thrill? She's alive. I would have returned before you came, but I had emergency surgery. I took nothing from her that can't be replaced with a few credits."

"You're not helping your case."

Sweat beaded the doctor's brow. "I've offered drugs. I can pay you. I'll give you what I got for the implants. Revenge won't undo what I did. Please. I have patients who need me—"

Miles slammed a metal fist onto the desk, cracking the wood. "Do I have your attention? First, the ends don't justify the means. Ever. And second, there was a transponder with the woman you operated on. I need it."

"I'm confused. She had nothing on her. I'm sure the scrappers took whatever this radio is. What's so important about it?"

Miles resisted the urge to hit the desk again. Intimidation had its limits. "They said to check with you. Someone's lying."

"They found her. She was already unconscious. I rebandaged her burner wounds, but they weren't life threatening. Then I got busy. Her implants pay the bills, not old shuttle components."

He was a good actor, or he didn't know.

Miles lowered the barrel of the burner. "I'm going to check the scrappers again, assuming they haven't been arrested or haven't run away. If you have the transponder, I'm the least of your worries."

The doctor nodded cautiously. "I'm telling you the truth, dog. I'm not interested in pocket change or personal belongings. The deal is I get their hardware, that's it. The scrappers get a cut from me later once I make my sale."

"How many?"

"You mean how much do I make?"

"No. I don't care about that. How many cyborgs have you waylaid?"

The doctor only shook his head. His lip quivered.

He doesn't remember.

Miles' grip tightened on the weapon. But then he holstered it and left the office.

Chapter Twenty-Six

The receptionist watched him with raw indignation as he stepped back into the waiting room. His phone was pulsing. Miles was hoping she'd say something, anything so he could explode and let her know about the monster for which she was working. A chill ran down his spine. What if the doctor wasn't the only one who helped the clinic get its funding?

Waiting patients glanced up at him. And what might they be here for? Cancer treatment? Pain management? An ulcer, an infection, the setting of a bone? One person's misery was another's salvation. How many would leave if they knew?

Santabutra Sin was calling.

"This is Miles."

"Kim, wherever you are, you need to move. They have your location. Get rid of your phone!"

The line went dead.

Miles paused next to a waste basket. But instead of discarding the device, he slipped it into a pocket.

Two electric motorcycles pulled up in front of the clinic. Not militia. Then he saw both drivers. They wore overalls and were identical to the man he had fought outside the café at the university. Each man removed a toolbox from the back of their bike. To anyone else watching, they were maintenance workers showing up for a repair.

How had they tracked him, and how had Santabutra known?

No time for that. One spotted Miles.

To the receptionist behind the glass, he asked, "Did you call the Yellow Tigers on me?"

She shook her head.

"Then do it now."

Miles drove a metal fist through the glass. It exploded into harmless fragments as he vaulted the desk, shoving the receptionist to the floor as he went. He had the burner out and popped up, only to duck again as a dart whizzed past.

"Everybody stay down!"

He crawled into the rear hallway. Too many people standing about. It didn't matter what kind of dart guns the attackers were using. If they had grenades or more bombs, the place was going to turn into a bloodbath. But if they were using darts, they wanted him alive.

"Take cover!" he shouted.

Crawling to the corner, he got into a crouch, readied his burner, and leaned out to aim.

One man was at the door. Insight tried to target. A flash popped from the man's eyes, then Miles' visual overlay went haywire. Suddenly, he had target windows filling his field of vision. He ducked back and tried to blink it away, but it was no use.

He could barely see as patients and staff scrambled past. The man would be on him in seconds.

"Insight off! Insight off!"

His eyes cleared as the man in overalls strode around the corner and aimed the dart gun. Miles sprang at him, his right arm raised defensively. The dart gun coughed. The projectile sheared off a finger and just missed Miles' face. His burner spun out of his grip. Miles punched the man with a left across the face. It was like punching a wall. Barely fazed, the man backhanded Miles and knocked him to the floor.

Miles tried to raise his right arm to deflect what was coming, but the man was too fast. The blow landed, and Miles felt the world turning as he dropped to the floor.

People were screaming. A fire alarm wailed.

The man stepped over Miles, was doing something in his toolkit which was strung around his shoulder. Miles fumbled about, searching for the burner. His left hand grasped the shaft of the bolt sticking out of his cybernetic hand. He tugged it out and stabbed the man in the calf. The man grunted before prying Miles' hand away from the makeshift weapon and pulling the bolt free. He had produced a device from the toolkit and switched it on. But then the man paused, let out a sigh, and keeled over.

Miles fought to regain his senses. He scrambled back against a wall and stood. Dr. Brook peered out from his room.

"Help me," Miles said.

"Who is that?"

"A bad guy. Might be here for both of us. He wasn't alone, and I can't fight another one."

He picked up the burner. Something had happened to it when his hand had been struck by the dart; it wouldn't power up.

"You have any weapons?"

The doctor shook his head. "This is a hospital."

"Then do you have a back door?"

Meridian had come out on top of the corporate shakedowns, mergers, and acquisitions during the generations in which Earth had migrated to the rest of the solar system. Safety had been a source of gallows humor for generations. If someone in another section of a habitat wasn't calling you back, they were in the loo, their coms weren't working, or their portion of the hab was taking a break and depressurizing for a spell.

Things had gotten a little better with safety after the return. Hospitals were supposed to have multiple fire exits, and the Bright Blocks clinic was no different.

Dr. Brook opened a trapdoor to a rusty ladder going down.

"What about my staff? The patients?"

"Should have thought about that when considering how you funded the place. Start climbing."

Miles monitored the hallway and the downed man while Dr. Brook descended the ladder. A nurse was taking cover beside a standing scale. She had her device out and was repeatedly jabbing the screen with her finger.

"It's not working!" she cried.

A quick check of his own phone confirmed it. No signal. The Meridian agents, or whoever they were, had set up a jammer. He hurried to follow the doctor.

The ladder let down into an alley near the parking lot. A metal sheet on hinges acted as a door leading to the market. The doctor was hurrying ahead of Miles and not waiting, but Miles caught up and clamped a hand on his arm.

"Let go of me!" the doctor yelled.

"You're not leaving my sight until we figure this out."

"You brought assassins to my hospital!"

"If I found you, they would have too. Stop squirming. Let's go back and take your bike. I'm sure it's faster than mine."

The motorcycle was a risk. The agents chasing them might know or soon discover what the doctor drove. But Miles didn't like their prospects of fleeing on foot, especially if the militia was also out to grab them.

They straddled the seat and the doctor got them going, weaving carefully through the crowd.

Miles kept his eye open for militia vehicles. His cybernetic hand remained unresponsive, but at least he could hang on to the doctor. He tried all the mental tricks to shut down the phantom pain from his severed finger.

"Your workshop, doc. Where is it?"

Dr. Brook drove them past the school. The crossing guard was gone. He sped up. "Where is what?"

"You must have a place where you keep your cybernetic prizes. A bolt hole? A shop?"

"You're talking about my home. They might know about that."

"Head there."

"Didn't you hear what I said, dog? If they found me at the hospital, they know who I am."

"That's a risk I'm willing to take. Those boys are heavily modded. And if I was a betting man, I'd guess you have something in your toolkit for taking care of that kind of problem."

Chapter Twenty-Seven

"That's a lot of junk."

Miles entered the massive container and ran his hands along the rack of dangling prosthetics. Arms, legs, partials of either, along with fragments of metal and plastic implants, made for a macabre display. A workbench with a pegboard adorned with an array of tools stood beneath it all. A chair, lights, soldering stand, clamps, wires, and boxes of circuits—the shop appeared to have everything.

"We can't wait here," Dr. Brook said. "If they're coming, there's no back exit. Let's get on the bike and leave. We have a head start. I don't know what you're planning, but this is no good. Dog?"

Miles inspected a few of the limbs. Most were old, barely much better than scrap. Others appeared newly constructed, perhaps current projects. So which pieces had belonged to Dawn? Or had the doctor done as he had said and sold them?

"This is where we need to be, doctor."

"You want me to fix your hand?"

"I doubt we have time. My Insight module is going haywire. Reboot isn't working."

Dr. Brook went to a tablet computer and turned it on. "That's not quick, either. How did that happen?"

"The men after us are enhanced. One of them flashed me with his eyes, and it sent my targeting into a tizzy."

"Laser scrambler. Nothing new, but one small enough to be a discreet implant?"

"The things they make these days, right?"

"I've started my program. It's going to take a minute. It will request access. You'll have to allow it. Unless you have a jack under your hair."

Miles had inert jacks hidden behind his right ear. "I'm not that old. I've been down this road. Do you have anything you might have used in procuring additional parts?"

Dr. Brook sounded distracted as he worked on the tablet. "What do you mean?"

"Finding unwilling candidates who would donate their limbs to your little enterprise."

"You think all these limbs are stolen? I've recovered these from scrappers. Some purchased for a few credits from family after the death of the owner. My work has helped hundreds of Bright Block and Seraph residents."

"Save me the speech. Dawn Moriti wasn't your first victim. The scrapyard guys knew to call you. So what if you had a cyborg who wasn't coming quietly?"

"You want a weapon to use against those men?"

"Turnabout's fair play. Plus, now that there's two of us, how can we lose?"

"By them showing up and shooting us. You don't have a weapon?"

"I dropped my burner back at the hospital. So what do you have?"

Dr. Brook rummaged about in a drawer. He produced something which looked like a flare gun. "Popper will fry most electronics. Single shot. You said there were two of them?"

Miles took the weapon and examined it. He hadn't seen a popper in decades. And while Insight wasn't awake to give him the rundown, popper ordinance was an old-school anti-bot measure before the Meridian war industry reasoned it was cheaper and easier to give its soldiers slug throwers and burners that would kill everything. But sometimes when you wanted to zap a spider drone without blowing holes in the walls of a habitat, a popper was the right tool.

Dr. Brook shifted in place as if he were ready to bolt. "Assuming the popper still works, you haven't told me what we're planning on doing about the second one. And if there're more..."

"Let me worry about that."

The doctor bit his lip. "Or, you keep the popper and the workshop, and I get out of here."

"There's a reason I pulled the main fuse off your motorcycle. If you're going to leave, it's on foot. Now sit down and let's get my head on straight."

Miles set his device on the workbench. Wished he could replay Santabutra's phone call, but he recalled her last words well enough.

Get rid of your phone.

Disabling the network chip would be simple enough. Then the Meridian agents wouldn't be able to find him.

The man in overalls was something Meridian had talked about being in the works ever since the war. No visible modifications, yet strong, resilient, and loaded to the gills. Laser eyes, muscle and skeletal implants, better and brighter chips in the brain box—which gram of excised tissue was the one which would make someone no longer human?

He reached for his device. Hesitated.

Santabutra had already risked much by contacting him. But how had she known his device was being tracked? That the agents could remotely hack a phone wasn't surprising. With Meridian, all things were possible. But one thing was certain. If they were coming for him and the doctor, it meant they didn't have what they were looking for.

It made Lucien Khar's prospects grim.

Sitting and waiting violated every ounce of training and all his instincts. It was the last minute, head-on plans that got people killed. If only he had other options.

He realized he was wrapping his fingertips on the workbench.

"A few more minutes," Dr. Brook said.

The phone screen lit up. Incoming call. But before Miles could pick up his device, a voice spoke as the call connected. Soft, male, devoid of emotion.

"Miles Kim? Can you hear me?"

"Who is this?"

"Surely you know. We just missed each other at the hospital."

"If by just missed you mean easily sidestepped you, then yeah, I guess I know who you are. You're one of the Meridian bounty hunters who's off the range and getting people hurt. Was it you or your associate whose ass I kicked?"

"While I find your levity inappropriate, I am happy we have a chance to speak. You have something of ours. This is your opportunity to come forward."

Miles couldn't help but notice the implied 'or else.' "And if I don't, assuming I even know what you're talking about? Going to tear through Seraph looking for me? More bombs? More shootouts on busy streets?"

The stranger's words were ice. "You play the fool. We will find you sooner than you think. You will regret not being forthcoming. But I will repeat my request. Hand over the transponder, and all this trouble goes away."

"Transponder? Huh. And here I was thinking it was just a broken radio. But if it's worth all this fuss, surely it's also worth some credits."

"If compensation is what you're after, that can be arranged. Let's meet."

"Credits are good. But how about letting me talk to Lucien Khar first?"

Some rustling on the stranger's line. "He is not with me at the moment."

"That's my first condition before we meet. Proof of life. And don't even try to fool me with a voice synth. If you've read up on my model of ear implants, you know I'm top of the line, and I'll hear the difference. Call back when you have Lucien and he can talk. Otherwise, you're wasting my time."

The screen to his device flickered and the call ended, all without Miles having to touch it.

"How did they do that?" Dr. Brook asked. "How did they do that with your phone?"

"Found an exploit in Seraph net, I'm guessing, along with the phone carrier signal. Have you remembered anything about a radio or transponder?"

"No, I swear. There wasn't anything like that when we found your friend."

Miles picked up his device. History showed no incoming calls. Everything else on the phone appeared to be functioning as normal.

"Well, doc, then it's going to get complicated. They think we have it, and they won't be giving up until they get it. "

"Then we run. What other choice is there?"

"We're not running. Finish up with me. Because it's time we get ready for company."

Chapter Twenty-Eight

Insight rebooted without a hitch. Miles hated how much he missed having it back on.

He blinked twice, brought up a browser search screen, blinked again, targeted about Dr. Brook's workshop, and then cleared his vision.

His device sat on the workbench where he had left it. If the Meridian agents were tracing it, they had his location and would arrive at any moment. Leading them on and pretending he had the transponder was a calculated risk. The doubts grew with every passing moment.

With the popper in hand, he had one chance to disable the first one through the door. Then he would need to disarm his victim and convince the other, or others, he had more poppers. Bluffing wasn't something he liked to do. Never play with cards you aren't holding. Even better, skip on the card games, cover your ass, and call for backup.

But he didn't want to bring anyone else in who would be implicated in everything he was facing with the law, along with the corporate assassins looking to take back a piece of wartime tech he didn't have.

"Doc, maybe you should get out of here."

Dr. Brook looked up from where he was taking cover behind a metal cabinet. "What do you mean? They're out there, aren't they? They're watching and waiting, and you want to use me as bait."

"Maybe. But unless they're flying, they have to deal with the same traffic conditions. You have a few minutes. Go, take cover outside, and when the shooting starts, run."

"You're crazy, dog. This is crazy. I'm sorry any of this ever happened. I'm so sorry."

Dr. Brook wasn't going anywhere. Maybe not as dumb as Miles thought. The notion the Meridian agents would just wait outside hadn't even crossed Miles' mind. Stupid oversight. Sleep deprivation was taking its toll, and here he was making tactical decisions with lives on the line.

The whine of the electric motorcycles was impossible to miss. Both engines cut out. Miles used the workbench for cover and readied the popper. Insight confirmed the effective range was the distance to the door. If the agents were cooperative, they'd bunch up so he could hit both of them, assuming it was just the two he had encountered at the Bright Blocks hospital.

When the puck-shaped grenade came flying into the workshop, Miles had time to duck. The ear-shattering pop and blinding flash shook the enclosed space of the cargo container, deafening him and leaving smudge marks across his vision despite his closed eyelids.

He popped back up to a kneeling position and blinked away the globby afterimages. Someone appeared in the doorway. He squeezed the popper's trigger. A muted crack and a trail of burned air. Miles pulled the trigger again and again, but nothing else happened. As advertised, the popper was a single shot munition. Yet the shape remained standing.

As the image cleared, he saw it was indeed one of the agents, perhaps the same one he had fought in the hallway. The man in overalls clung to the door of the container. He was convulsing. Finally, a seizure ran through his body, then he pitched forward. A dart gun tumbled from his hands. Miles raced for it, keeping his head down as he snatched it up.

Movement outside. Behind the two bikes, the other agent in identical garb pulled something out of a tool kit resting on the ground. A spider unfolded, sprouting legs. The drone adjusted itself before skittering towards Miles.

Miles grabbed the door and pulled it shut. The downed agent's foot was in the way. The spider bot slammed into the door. Metal fingers stabbed through the opening, but Miles maneuvered himself so it couldn't reach him.

"Stop this foolishness and surrender," the agent called. "You can't escape. This only prolongs the inevitable."

While gripping the door, Miles tried to target the bot. But as he angled the dart gun so the barrel was aiming out the opening, a bright spark from one of the spider's fingers sent a shivering jolt through the weapon, forcing Miles to drop it. When he went to pick it up, a leg slashed at his hand, forcing him to pull his arm back.

It pushed the door in.

"Doc..."

Miles planted both feet and leaned hard, but the spider was too strong. "Doc!"

But Dr. Brook wasn't coming out of his hiding place behind the cabinet.

The spider got two legs against the frame of the cargo container and two inside the door. Miles felt himself losing ground as his boots slid.

A fire extinguisher was clipped to the nearby wall. Miles grabbed for it. The door slammed open, almost knocking him down, but he snatched the extinguisher from the wall, turned it on the spider, pulled the pin, and squeezed the discharge lever.

Nothing happened. The spider leaped. With a swing of the extinguisher, Miles batted it down. He drove the canister into it once, twice, a third time, and heard the satisfying *pop* of something breaking. The machine went limp.

The second agent appeared at the door. When Miles flung the extinguisher, the man deflected it with a forearm and raised a weapon. The dart struck a crate as Miles dove for cover.

The Meridian agent's voice remained eerily calm. "Stop this foolishness and surrender."

"You take another step inside and it'll cost you!"

Miles looked around for anything that would serve as an impromptu weapon. The tools and workbench were too far away. Yet the agent hesitated, using the door as cover. The popper had taken his partner down. Miles might have more. But he didn't.

"We're going to wait here until the militia comes," Miles said. "You ready for that? Going to shoot it out with them?"

"You're making a mistake. Our patience with you is finished. Give us the transponder."

"I told you what I want. Until I get to talk to Lucien—"

A sharp crack from behind him. Miles pitched forward, convulsing.

The doctor stooped over him, a second popper in hand. "I'm sorry. It was the only way." He straightened and raised his hands. "I have him. I got him for you. We give up, and he can tell you where your transponder is!"

Chapter Twenty-Nine

Miles kept his eyes shut as hands grabbed and dragged him into a waiting vehicle, a van or small box truck. He was dropped onto a bare metal bed, his wrists and ankles zip tied. The agents rarely spoke, and when they did, it was always a curt command to another agent. Miles counted at least three of them, and judging by the sounds, a fourth agent was the one he had shot with the popper.

Insight's start-up prompt waited.

He strained his ears for any sign of what happened to Dr. Brook. Would he be executed, taken, or left behind? But the driver wasn't waiting on the others and started the van and drove off.

The doctor had done as Miles had asked. Now, would he keep his mouth shut, or let on that the second popper was nothing more than a blank, a ruse?

As much as the agents could run rough-shod through Seraph, the threat of the militia surely would concern them, as a full response meant a shootout the agents couldn't hope to win. They wanted their precious device, and Miles banked on the fact they needed to talk to him someplace private. That someplace might be where they had taken Lucien Khar.

Miles' arm and legs grew numb. The tingling ran up through both shoulders. His hips complained by the time they stopped. Even with Insight off, Miles guesstimated they had driven some five kilometers, much of it over the rougher roads of the outlying districts of Seraph. But finally the vehicle paused and waited as a door to a building rolled up and they drove inside.

The driver dragged him out of the back of the van, dropping him hard on concrete.

"Oof!"

"He's awake."

Miles opened his eyes. Two of the agents looked down at him. One wore the overalls, the other a head-to-toe black haptic suit with a helmet. They were inside an unremarkable warehouse or garage with a high ceiling, naked ductwork, and metal shelving along the walls. The smell of old oil and the traces of solvent fumes permeated.

They both took hold of his shoulders and dragged him down a ramp into a sublevel. Cables and conduits covered the walls. A hydraulic system stood in the center of the gloomy chamber. But the room was a mechanic's pit with no ceiling, no doubt meant to service whatever vehicles would pull over it

Lucien Khar sat strapped to a chair, his head slumped. His face looked puffy and bruised. Dried blood crusted his nose and mouth. Miles couldn't tell if he was breathing.

The agents unceremoniously dumped Miles atop a pile of rags.

"No noise," the one in overalls said before they both headed off up the ramp.

Miles twisted and rolled in an attempt to sit up. The numbness creeping through his limbs didn't help. If they saw he was fully alert and not stunned, they might drug him or restrain him further. But he needed to know if Lucien was still alive.

He strained his ears. The van started up again. The engine faded, and the *whirr* of a metal door made enough noise that Miles took the chance.

"Lucien? Lucien? Wake up!"

Nothing.

The vibrating sounds rose to a crescendo.

"Lucien Khar!"

The young man's eyes fluttered. He shook his head weakly, blinked a few times, and glanced about as if unable to see Miles. His dry, cracked lips moved before he whispered, "It's you."

"Yeah," Miles whispered back. "I'm here to get you out."

Lucien shook his head. "C-can't. You can't. Don't do anything." His voice grew louder. "He'll hurt me."

"Shh! Keep calm. I'm getting us both away from here alive. Can you move at all?"

"No, I can't." His eyes went wide as he looked about. It was only then that Miles saw electrodes planted into the back of Lucien's head. Implants? What were the agents doing to him?

But even without Insight's help, Miles recalled the rumors of tech Meridian intelligence services had used on prisoners, ways of accessing thoughts and tearing memories free from an unwilling subject. Between the drugs and the process, it left the victim's psyche shattered, if not outright killing them.

Rumors, only rumors. Yet here it was as plain as day.

The plastic bindings on his wrist resisted him as he strained against them. He wiggled his metal arm enough where he might bust the bindings, but without leverage, he only succeeded in sawing the sharp plastic into the flesh of his left wrist. The material was too thick.

From above, the garage was quiet. The man in the haptic suit returned, walking down the ramp with purpose.

Miles closed his eyes and set his head down.

The Meridian agent kneeled beside him. Fingers prodded his eye and the side of his face. Then a sharp pain surged through his skull.

"Ah, you're awake." The man's voice was the same as the one on the phone. Tranquil. Almost dreamy. "No doubt in pain. Can you hear me? Your ears appear intact. I need to know if we can communicate."

Miles looked up at him. "I hear you."

"Good. Our purpose is to retrieve a transponder. Do you understand the request?"

"I speak English. Yes, I understand. I have conditions—"

The agent touched the side of Miles' face again. The pain was instant, white hot, and caused Miles to cry out. The man moved a forefinger before Miles' eyes. The glove had wires running along its vinyl-like surface. The entire suit appeared to be meant for some kind of full immersion simulation.

"That is a foretaste of what you will experience soon. Am I speaking loud enough?"

"I hear you. But you're not going to get what you want this way."

"It is more time consuming, but effective. Necessary, too, as you are reluctant to share the simplest of information. One last time: where is our transponder?"

"Let us both walk and I'll tell you where I hid it—nggggg!"

The third shock ran from his skull through his neck and woke up every sleeping nerve in his limbs, sending lightning through his fingertips and toes. The vision in his right eye lit up like a supernova. He smelled skin burning. And when the sensation stopped a second or a day later, his body went slack and every muscle went to jelly.

He moaned.

The agent came and went, attaching small wires to Miles' head that ran to a junction box with a router sporting four stubby antennae. Through it all, Lucien's head once again had lolled forward.

Miles' throat felt raw. "I prefer a light gun oil on the joints. Bearing grease is too goopy and leaves a residue. Leaves marks on the sheets. And while you're working, I lost a finger. The entire hand needs the joints adjusted. They get stiff when the weather gets cold."

"Charming. Your strength would best serve you by telling us what we need to know."

"And like I said, you won't get what you want this way. The mesh between my Insight module and my brain won't allow it. Insight isn't running, and it will knock me out if you try to jumpstart it. You'll learn nothing."

Was that the faintest smile on the agent's face? "We will see."

The agent left Miles' side and vanished up the ramp. After some clattering about above them, the garage went quiet except for the hum of what sounded like a machine turning on.

With the electrodes on his head, Miles had no doubts about what would follow. A brute force attempt at what was inside his head and anything his Insight module could tell them. The only chance he had was the hope that they still believed the computer side of his mind remained knocked out by the popper. But getting shocked again meant he'd be truly out of it.

So he turned Insight on and let the agent see everything.

Chapter Thirty

The electronic fingers plying Miles' mind weren't gentle. They pushed and probed and jabbed without care, causing Miles to involuntarily flinch.

Insight was finishing up its reboot. The agent must have noticed, because the prickling sensations stopped. No doubt the agent had expected the need to knock the doors down to Miles' stored memories, and now found them wide open.

It was risky, but the only play Miles had left, if they were to stand any chance to escape.

It meant the agent would soon know that Miles had never set his eyes on the transponder, that the doctor likewise didn't know, and that Dawn Moriti was still alive. They'd also have her location. The thought that at any moment more of the agents might return only underscored how quickly Miles needed to act.

While the agent sifted through the glut of information, he might miss what happened next.

Miles torqued his metal arm. The limb which was supposed to be neutralized worked back and forth against the ties holding it. Miles gritted his teeth as the sawing motion dug the sharp plastic further into his left wrist. His "real" arm was soon slick with blood. He tried his best not to cry out, not to even think about what was happening. A stray sound or an uncensored thought would betray him, and the agent would put a stop to his actions. But with a final twist, the binding popped.

He flexed both hands, fighting to get the feeling back, but resisted the urge to yank the electrodes from his head. Snapping the bindings off his ankles was simple enough with his metal fingers. He rose, wobbly on his feet, and had enough slack in the cords attached to him to make it to Lucien's side.

Lucien's eyes were open.

Miles tapped a finger to his lips. Whispered, "You're going to have to try to walk. No sound." He worked to free Lucien from the chair. Zip ties on each arm and leg had held him fast, and all his limbs were ragged with abrasions, a testament to his having struggled through his sessions with the interrogator.

Lucien surprised Miles when he stood without needing help. His eyes were suddenly wide with panic. Miles thought he would cry out or try to run even as he was still attached to the cables wiring his head.

"Get them out!" Lucien hissed.

Miles didn't dare yank them free. Too great a risk of injury. But not being able to tell quickly how they connected to the young man's skull and the skin, he found a link in the cord which easily detached with a simple pinch. Soon Lucien had three cables dangling around his neck like plastic hair extensions. When Miles tried to find similar segments to free himself, there were none.

His Insight module paged through recent sights and sounds. While memories weren't exactly video and audio, they were solid impressions, especially of recent events. The agent would have what he needed soon. The faintest electrical tickle ran through his head.

"Help me get these off," Miles whispered.

Lucien examined Miles' scalp. "I can't. I don't see how."

Miles searched the ground around the chair. Strewn rubbish filled the corners of the tight space. The cables connecting him ran to the router. But power cords were sloppily bundled and dangled freely as they ran up to whatever machines the agent was using for his work.

The electric tingle grew in intensity.

A rough disconnect could injure or kill him. But even if he discovered a tool to sever the cord, the shock to his brain implant might prove disabling.

"Run," Miles said. "Get out of here. Don't go home. Don't call anyone you know."

"I can't."

The simple statement made Lucien sound like a boy afraid of falling off his bicycle. It was also too loud.

From above them, the agent asked, "What are you doing, Miles Kim?"

The man appeared at the edge of the pit, his head and arms wired like a marionette. The tops of whatever stack of computer equipment stood just behind him.

Miles grabbed the bundled power cords with both arms and, using his legs, he heaved with all his might. The unsecured cables tugged hard on the equipment, then the tower toppled, slamming against the agent and sending it all down into the pit to crash around Miles.

The Meridian agent fought to rise, the rack trapping him below the waist and pinning one arm. But Miles was on him, slamming him repeatedly in the face until he stopped moving. He checked him for weapons and found a needle pistol.

"How many more of you people are there?" Miles asked the agent. When the man didn't answer, Miles tore away the goggles and mask.

The man had pasty skin and a bloody lip from the fall. But his eyes were a soft blue and didn't appear enhanced. Miles could only hope he was correct, lest he get zapped by another cyborg zapper embedded inside an eyeball.

"Get away from him," Lucien Khar said. "He might have blades on him."

The agent coughed. Winced in pain. "Miles Kim. Record redacted or deleted. Still present on classified documents. You have a duty to your corporation, sergeant."

Miles stepped on the agent's free hand. If he had finger blades or another concealed weapon, he wouldn't be able to use it. "I'm retired. What did you come all this way for? What's this transponder?"

"It's the future. Seraph, New Pacific, every other scattered town and community—they'll be begging to return to the fold."

"Why just Meridian? If it's important enough, shouldn't everyone have it?"

"You'd have us fight another war, one of words, where we squabble about whethers and shoulds. With one swift action, we can take back what was lost."

"You're not making any sense."

"He's stalling," Lucien said.

The agent shook his head. "My fellow operatives won't be back for hours. They know I need my silence, and they will leave no stone unturned in their search. But know that your son will need to be questioned, along with any other acquaintance. Tell me you know where the transponder is. Stop the violence. Do your duty."

Miles moved to get himself away from the wreckage.

"Where are you going?" the agent asked.

"Out of here. I'm getting Lucien here to safety, and then I'm going to make sure my son's okay. If I see you again, I'm going to kill you. Pass it along to the rest of your squad."

"You can't go. Where is it, Sergeant Kim?"

Miles stumbled when he tried to walk away. Part of the fallen rack pinned the cords attached to Miles' head.

Lucien stooped next to him. "I'll pull it free. You lift. Give me the gun."

Miles handed it over without thinking. When Lucien shot the agent, Miles hit the floor, raising his hands in a defensive gesture which would do nothing to protect him at such a close range. Lucien fired a half-dozen more times. The agent was cut to pieces.

"That takes care of that," Lucien said. He turned the weapon on Miles. "I owe you a thank you, I guess. But you're a problem."

Miles showed his hands. "You got him. We can go. What are you doing?"

"My father told me I needed to be more decisive. I'm going to leave before more of them come back. But I want to know something. You came all this way to get me out. Why?"

"Because it's what I do."

"Looking for a piece of the pie just like everyone else, aren't you? If my father taught me anything, it's never to share."

"I want nothing from you. I let myself be caught to get you out of their hands. You have nothing to do with this."

The needle gun held steady. "How would you know?"

"Because you told me yourself you were scared when the shooting started at the meeting. All you wanted to do was run. If you knew what your father and the other two were hoping to buy and how valuable it was, you would have gone inside to save it."

"You're just another stupid cop. I know what my dad was there for. He wouldn't shut up about it. All this talk about taking control from the Caretakers, and how much money he was going to make."

Miles tugged on the wires. He remained held fast.

Lucien watched him with unmasked annoyance. "You really think it's just a radio, don't you? It's an IFF transponder. It's programed with the algorithm to bypass detection from any of the Caretaker orbital sensors."

"You really believe they're still up there watching or care if something flying is identified as friendly?"

"You mean are they listening? Doesn't matter what I think, but my dad believed. Said Meridian has kept close watch and was waiting for an opportunity like the IFF to make a move."

"Meridian has always claimed they don't know," Miles said.

"Sounds like you weren't in the loop. My dad spent a fortune keeping connected. Said Meridian intelligence *knows* they're still there. They've kept tabs on the Caretakers' orbital satellites as best as possible, but with the debris field, it's hard to know what's active and what isn't. But with the transponder data, it means whoever has it can go back up there."

The needle gun barrel lowered slightly, but Lucien hadn't taken his eyes off Miles. It was as if he were trying to make a choice. Then he put the weapon in his belt as if he were a thug in a serial.

Miles dared take a breath. "The other agents won't quit."

"Maybe. But they got elbow-deep into my brain. They know I don't have it. I get out of here, they might forget about me."

"You don't have it and you don't know where it is."

"More precisely, I don't care. Hope they go easy on you."

With that, Lucien Khar hurried up the ramp, leaving Miles to his fate.

Chapter Thirty-One

The agents were going to go after Dillan, and there was nothing Miles could do about it trapped in the garage. He again contemplated severing the cables connected to his head but knew he wouldn't do his son any good if he passed out or suffered a fatal shock.

He searched the fallen terminals, wishing for better light. Fumbling around and pushing the toppled rack aside, he groped until he found the router. One by one, he twisted and unplugged everything. The cables came free after some doing, but soon he had them wound around one arm like an oversized extension cord. Getting the last of it out from under the fallen rack became simple enough.

For good measure, he went through the dead agent's belongings. Nothing useful.

He fought a dizzy spell as he climbed the ramp. No vehicle. A door stood ajar. Lucien hadn't bothered closing it on his way out. Bright afternoon sunlight shined, blinding him. They were in a warehouse on a large lot, with no visible landmarks. Miles squinted and ignored the growing throbbing in his head.

A vehicle engine was coming closer.

The property had a fence some distance away. Miles could make the sprint but doubted his ability to climb. He ducked back inside and searched for anything which might serve as a weapon. The agent's work area was in disarray after most of the equipment had gone over into the hydraulic pit. But a toolbox identical to what the other agent carried stood beside a column. He discovered a fist-sized slug thrower inside. No palm print user lock. It was loaded. Miles flipped the safety off and took position behind a debris box and waited.

The rumble of the vehicle grew louder. It wasn't the agent's van, but something bigger. A militia tank, he decided. Sounds of hydraulics of heavy doors opening were followed by the thud of boots.

A sharp rap at the door. "Seraph militia. We have a warrant."

Miles didn't move. Which militia? And what did it mean for him?

The voice from outside boomed over a suit amplifier. "Seraph militia! Come out now!"

"I'm here," Miles called. "Identify your name, rank, and company."

"Come to the door and we can show you ID."

"Negative. Name, rank, and company."

Reflections in the windows high above the door showed there were at least three troopers ready to blast, smash, or burn their way in.

"Miles Kim?" Sheriff Vaca called over the vehicle's speaker.

He hoped they had an amplified microphone. He didn't feel up to shouting. "Yeah, it's me. I have a dead Meridian agent in here. I'm not surrendering to them."

"They're not with us. We're trying to stop any more violence. Come to the door."

At least she could hear him. "How did you find me?"

"Your device. We tracked it."

His phone? It wasn't on him. He had searched the dead agent. Keeping the pistol raised, he went to the toolbox. Dumped it. There was his device. Was there anyone *not* tracking it? A tidbit he filed away when it came time to write a product review.

He called Dillan. It went to voicemail. Called again.

He barely flinched when the troopers outside smashed the door off its hinges and stormed in, burner rifles aiming and shouting at him to drop his weapon and lie down.

"My son—" he said when one of them slammed the butt of their gun against his skull, knocking him to the ground.

His hands were once again fastened behind his back. The Red Banner cops swept through the place, going over every inch. Sheriff Vaca appeared above him, hands clasped behind her back, her jaw clenched and her eyes intent.

"It's not here," Miles said.

"How do you know?"

"Because the dead Meridian agent down in the pit was still asking. Lucien Khar doesn't have it, either. It's in the wind. It's over."

"Forgive me if I don't take your word for it. You have a lot to answer for. Assault. Impeding an investigation. You're an accomplice in a shooting which injured two sworn peace officers. You trespassed on militia property and aided in the escape of a material witness and suspect of numerous crimes. You're at the center of this. It's nowhere near over."

"They know about my son. Threatened him. I need to see if he's safe."

"Where's Lucien Khar?"

So Lucien had escaped. "I'm not talking to anyone except the marshal."

"You don't get to make requests."

"Suit yourself. I'm also not talking until you get me unhooked from these cables."

A pair of medics appeared after a few minutes and got him sitting up. They patted him down before they started the careful work of removing the probes stabbing his brain. He flinched with each tug until they finally got them all out, only to drive staples into his head with no warning. Finally, a medic applied a first aid gel, which numbed everything.

His throat felt parched. His left wrist was on fire and sticky with blood, and he was afraid it was broken from his escape from the zip tie. One cop had his phone. It chimed. He handed it to the sheriff.

"Is that Dillan?"

Vaca ended the call and put her phone into a jacket pocket. "We know what you want. And you know what *I* want."

"You can't do this. He's in danger."

"If he's experiencing an emergency, he can call the Seraph public safety number."

"Meridian isn't playing around. Haven't you lost enough people?"

"We're hunting their agents as we speak. You did our job for us with that one down there. Tell me where the transponder is."

"I told you I don't know. Why does the Seraph sheriff care so much about an IFF unit made for a space shuttle?"

She arched an eyebrow. "Someone's been talking. What else do you know?"

"Not much, except even if that thing works, there's no reason to believe the Caretakers haven't changed their codes."

"You think you're clever believing that. Of course they did, assuming they're still alive. But with it, the code's algorithm can be cracked."

Miles tried to adjust himself to ease the pain in his arms and shoulders. Whatever magic the gel had worked didn't extend beyond his scalp. "You don't really care about it either, do you? Neither did Lucien. But you're here leading the charge. So who's paying you to steamroll through Seraph? It's pretty clear Bing Patton has people in the Yellow Tigers in the loop, and you don't get along with them, considering your current company. That leaves Xander Trowbridge or Shahid Khar, but Lucien, for all his faults, hid little when I asked. He didn't mention you. So I'm thinking that rules out his father."

"Aren't you bright? You can stay as smug as you want when we throw you into one of our detention tanks for a few weeks while we sort this out. Unless, of course, you change your mind and suddenly remember something. Give me the location of the transponder, or the fish who got away. She knows, doesn't she?"

Miles remained mute. The medics hauled him to his feet and escorted him to the back of the waiting tank. Miles felt the gnawing ache in his gut grow as he thought about what the agents might do to Dillan.

One medic began packing the Meridian equipment into the back next to him.

"Just in case we need to get creative," the medic said with a wink before closing the rear compartment.

Chapter Thirty-Two

Miles had time to contemplate his fate as the tank engine rumbled to life and the sheriff, along with her squad, piled in.

Meridian Corporation had always used its own special investigation unit that would occasionally throw their weight around and take over a sensitive case. The River City cops, along with the army MPs, had no choice but to stand back and let it happen.

Seraph wasn't the same, but it wasn't much different.

He'd be tossed in a cell and allowed to stew. Perhaps the sheriff would have him executed once she got what she was after. He could easily give her Dawn. Might save Dillan. But no, he realized, no matter what he shared, the sheriff was going to do what was good for her and her credit balance, and getting rid of a couple more bodies would be simpler than any alternative.

He would buy some time for Dawn, at least.

Had the Meridian agent learned Dawn's location from his brain scan? He assumed so. But picking through memories took time, and Miles had killed him before he could share anything.

The blast of sirens and a blaring flurry of horns preceded the sharp stab of the brakes, sending Miles hard against the wall of the tank's holding compartment. He struggled to sit upright, his cuffed wrists chained to a ring set in the floor. Some of the equipment had toppled. He craned his neck, but he couldn't get high enough to see out the slit windows.

The Red Banner cops deployed.

"Put down your weapons! Put down your weapons!" cried someone through a loudspeaker.

"Here we go again," Miles said. He kicked the barrier between the storage compartment and the passenger space beyond. "Hey, what's going on?"

"Be quiet," the sheriff said. Then her voice blared on the tank's own, even louder squawk box: "Yellow Tigers, this is Sheriff Vaca. Your units are out of line. Put down your weapons and get that runner out of the way, or you'll find yourself in violation of Seraph law."

"This is Marshal Barma. You're the one who needs to stand down. Your authority over this investigation is rescinded by order of Mayor Bedford."

The tank address system squealed once before shutting off. Even in the back compartment, he could hear the sheriff cursing a storm. Then a door opened. Her voice was audible outside, along with Barma's, as they shouted at each other. Miles couldn't get close enough to press his ear to the back doors, but he caught snippets.

From Sheriff Vaca: "In the middle of an active investigation," "Jeopardizing the safety of the city," and "Tigers almost started a shootout with a Red District squad."

Marshal Barma: "Can't declare martial law and act without city approval," "Not an autonomous force," and "This investigation is over until Mayor Bedford sees both of us in person. Now let my deputy go."

The back doors opened. A Yellow Tiger trooper brought Miles outside. Barma stood in the middle of the street with his fists on his hips, his hat tilted back, and his untucked shirt damp with sweat as he faced down the much smaller Vaca in her blue windbreaker. Three Yellow Tiger cruisers along with Barma's tiny subcompact were parked, blocking both lanes.

"We'll see about this, Barma," she said. "You'll regret it. Mark my words, you will."

She stormed through the line of the Red District cops and climbed back inside the tank. Barma motioned for Miles to be brought forward.

The trooper undid the cuffs. Miles immediately massaged his left wrist, careful to avoid the bloody lacerations in his skin.

Barma accepted Miles' hat and device from one of the Red District soldiers before handing them over. "One of your fingers is missing."

Miles tried to unlock his device but saw the screen had been smashed and wouldn't light up. "Parts have been falling off spontaneously lately. Not sure if there's a cure."

"You okay?"

"I need to call Dillan."

"Your son's safe. There's a Yellow Tiger unit watching him now at his work. We also picked up Lucien Khar. He's being taken home. The Tigers have a detail on him, too."

"Thought you were taking time off."

"Got bored last night. And this morning the wheels started turning. Couldn't let it lie."

"How'd you know where to find me, anyway? Red Banners tracked my phone. You use their radio or the traffic network?"

"Nothing that fancy. A couple of credits a month to their dispatcher, and I get a text message with whatever I need when I ask nicely."

"So what's up with this mayor thing? How did it get Vaca to back down?"

"Easy," Barma said. "Mayor Bedford is both our bosses. He gets final say on who gets what. If she can play that card, so can I. And after three shootouts across the city, a bombing, and a couple of kidnappings, he wants a clear picture of what's happening before letting anyone off the leash."

"I could have used your help earlier."

"Believe me when I say I'm busy. I have six marshals out on patrol who need support. I have one sick in the hospital, and another out on leave. But I'm not kidding. The mayor wants to see me and her."

Miles moved to block Barma from returning to his car. Meanwhile, the tank had revved up and the Yellow Tiger cruisers began to leave.

"How did you know to come out here at this particular time?" Miles asked.

"I was monitoring the situation. Then Captain Sin called and told me how deep you had gotten."

"And you got the Yellow Tigers to back you up."

Barma grinned. "Amazing what I can manage when I pull my weight."

"Or you got some extra motivation."

The grin vanished. "What are you implying?"

"It's been a long couple of days. I've been blown up, my Insight module fried, flash banged, my head stuck with electrodes, and my brain probed. See my hand? Someone busted my finger, and the only doctor I know here who works on cyborgs performs surgery on unwilling subjects. I'm past implying and jumping straight to accusations. You're involved in this in some way you don't want to share. I want to know what that is. Who's paying you?"

"You really want to do this in the middle of the street?"

There was traffic either waiting or edging past, with plenty of nasty stares from the angry drivers. If one of the Yellow Tiger cruisers wasn't lingering, there'd be blaring horns. Miles followed Barma into his car, and the marshal drove for a hundred meters to a turnout onto a dead field of dry grass. They were alone.

Miles spoke first. "You said you don't trust anyone. Now you show up with a writ from the mayor's office and the backing of one of the militias. Someone likes you suddenly, and you're trying to put a lid on this thing when it's still boiling over."

Barma was tapping the steering wheel with his thumb and looking straight ahead. At least wedged into his seat like that, Miles doubted the big man could even draw his weapon, if it came to that.

"A little gratitude would be nice," Barma said softly.

"That's not a denial. So how's the other shoe going to drop? I'm the last suspect who might have any idea where your transponder is. You have an interrogation center of your own? Back to Yellow Tiger HQ?"

"Geez, Kim, you have an imagination. No, nothing like that is coming your way. Looks like you could use a hospital, though. You don't actually know where this thing is, do you?"

"What makes you say that?" Miles asked.

"You're still alive. The Meridian agents were still looking."

"Were?"

"Yellow Tigers cornered them up in the Factory District. They didn't come quietly. After all their searching, they were empty-handed. This radio doohickey and everyone who was looking for it are gone, and that's for the better. It's over. You asked who's paying me? I work for Seraph."

"You're trying to make what you do sound noble."

"Someone authorizes the credits which show up in my account. But since you're not letting up, the Yellow Tiger organization made overtures to me yesterday. Their board is processing what Bing Patton was planning, and they decided they wanted to head a different direction. They want to make sure the radio thingy stays lost. Buried is better, broken is best. I checked with the mayor, and he agrees. So I took them up on the offer."

"A bribe."

"A bonus. What? You don't like that? Offend some lingering sense of propriety? You don't work here or for me anymore. I did you a solid."

"You're on the take. Even if it's for a little, someone tells you when to be and not be a cop."

"Seraph's an expensive town. I have bills."

"Don't we all?"

They sat for a moment.

Miles felt acid in his throat. "Doohickey? Do you even know what the transponder is?"

"No one's volunteered, and I don't want to know. Sheriff Vaca and Red District will stand down or lose everything. It's the way the wind's blowing. It's over."

"You think you got all the Meridian agents? They're no joke."

"I'm going back to where they found you and picking through everything. We're checking camera feeds to see if we missed any of them. If we did, it'll be time to form up an old-fashioned posse and hunt them down. There's pressure after everything that's happened to wrap this up. Seraph protects what it has, and word is out that Meridian has overstepped."

Barma started the car and drove back to the road.

Miles cradled his hurt wrist. "Where are you taking me?"

"Wood Creek Hospital or back to your hotel. You're done. You're also a mess."

"If it's just the same, take me to Bright Blocks."

Barma eyed him suspiciously. "You know something."

"Very little, it seems. But I like the clinic there, and it's also where I left my ride."

Chapter Thirty-Three

By the time Barma pulled into the lot below the Bright Blocks clinic, Miles had dozed off.

"Is this the place?" Barma asked.

Miles scanned the parked vehicles. His blue scooter was gone.

"Looks like I forgot where I parked it, or the locals appreciated my ride a little too much. It might be at my mechanic."

"You have a mechanic?"

"It's in the district here."

Miles gave directions and Barma took him to Doctor Brook's garage. The doctor's big motorcycle waited in a spot between the shipping containers.

"There she is," Miles said as he got out of the subcompact.

"Huh. Not a cheap ride. Take it easy, Miles."

Barma didn't wait around.

Was the doctor still alive? He paused at the door to the container. It stood ajar. From inside came Dr. Brook's voice.

"Be there in thirty minutes. That's the quickest I can make it. No, I know what happened and I don't know who those men were. It's nothing that can't be cleaned up. Get the report from the militia and I'll file it with the insurance as soon as I get in."

So their ploy with the Meridian agents had worked. Unfortunately for Dr. Brook, he was going to need more time to make his appointment.

Miles crouched next to the bike, opened the small fuse box, and fished the three fuses he had removed from his pocket. They were intact. They slipped in place easy enough, and he snapped the box closed and got on the bike, slipping the key into the ignition. The engine whined to life.

He sped off onto the road, the hot air licking his face.

Was this it? Was it like Barma had said, and the matter was over? The three junkyard deaths and all the other crimes swept under the rug by the Seraph mayor and his law enforcement agencies?

And what were the odds that the treasure the three wealthiest Seraph citizens were set to purchase would be forgotten?

Either Marshal Barma was naïve, or he was lying.

Miles didn't have money for a new phone. So he rode to Dillan's place of work. It was late enough in the afternoon he feared he might miss him. Out in front of the single-level school, he pulled up next to Zoe's tiny silver car. Other parents were likewise waiting, some on the sidewalks talking in groups, while several students biked and walked past. It was at least an hour after school had let out.

Zoe was out of her car and leaned in to hug him. "What are you doing here?"

"I thought I'd check in with Dillan."

"Okay. Although he's supposed to be out any minute, we're running late. We're doing an early dinner because we both have work. He has a dress rehearsal later with some of the parents present."

"I'm not here to keep him long. I just...needed to see him."

"Well, isn't that sweet?" She gave him a once-over. "What happened to you?"

"It was a rough day. I survived."

"Maybe I should see the other guy before passing judgement, but are you okay?"

"I'm fine. You talked to Dillan this afternoon?"

"Texted an hour ago. He's fine too. You should come with us. Get a bite. Maybe everyone's nerves will calm down. Then the two of you can talk, because it looks like you have something to get off your chest."

"You say he's good."

"Yeah. Miles, what's wrong? He's held up as usual, but he's fine. Call him, if you can't wait for him to come out."

"My phone stopped working. I just needed to hear from him he's all right. But if you just talked to him, then that's good enough. Maybe we'll all have dinner another night. I realize I'm a sight, and I need to go back to my hotel and get some rest."

"Offer's open. I'm sure he'll be happy to see you, if you just wait another minute."

A group of children who straggled past were better groomed than the students he had seen heading to school in Bright Blocks. While some were disheveled, none had holes in their clothes, and what they wore appeared to fit. The boys had trimmed hair, and some wore ball caps for the school cricket team, while a few of the girls already had touches of makeup and metal jewelry instead of plastic in gaudy colors.

"Miles?" Zoe said. "What's wrong?"

"Nothing." But he continued to watch the kids. An itch at the edge of his mind was trying to piece something together, but without Insight, it was hazy and difficult to grasp.

"I'm going to go."

"I'll tell Dillan you were here to say hello. By the way, nice bike."

He said goodbye and got his motorcycle moving. As Barma had told him, a Yellow Tiger officer waited in a cruiser at the entrance to the student pickup lane. The trooper looked bored.

Nothing was happening. Dillan was safe. Miles could return to his hotel, but he had one more stop to make.

Dawn Moriti's bungalow was empty. It was as if no one had ever lived there, the bed tidy and made, the bathroom spotless, the drugs and weapons gone.

Miles saw no scuffs on the floor, no sign the door had been smashed or the lock scraped up and picked. No blood spatters or broken furniture, either.

While it was possible the Meridian agents or some other operators had arrived and scooped her up, he doubted any of them would have bothered scrubbing up like this. It was her. And like her withdrawal from the scene of the shootout, he guessed she hadn't left a single trace of physical evidence of her presence because of whatever spy-level nanobots she must keep inside her sleeve.

He felt some measure of relief when he spotted the older neighbor outside watching him as he emerged. At least she hadn't eliminated all the eyewitnesses to her existence.

Miles could only guess whether she was truly gone. But would she once again try to reacquire the transponder, or would she cut her losses?

He went outside and found the neighbor. "Did you see Dawn leave this afternoon?"

The old man scowled as he considered Miles. "Don't suppose I did."

"I suppose you didn't, either. Or at least you're not going to tell me."

But Miles dropped it. Wasn't in the mood to brace the neighbor for more information. So what if he had seen her depart? It wasn't as if he could say where she was going.

Miles went back to his bike. Sat for a moment. The lumpy hotel bed sounded good. But twenty minutes later, he pulled onto Lucien Khar's street.

Two Yellow Tiger patrol cars were watching the place.

Miles pulled behind a dumpster. Lucien was home and safe. It was over. Yet something about the situation felt like when his drill instructor would shout them to silence following a minor row. Things would settle for an hour or a day, sure, but an unexpected elbow throw or a push off a training obstacle would remind everyone that sometimes the instructors weren't looking and a matter between recruits wasn't settled.

After a couple of hours and the sun having set, he realized he might be wrong. Santabutra Sin was probably wondering if he had abandoned his dog with her. His stomach growled. And Tristan was probably having kittens waiting for him to show up, assuming he still had a security job to return to.

There wasn't much traffic on the residential street. A few strollers. But otherwise it was a calm night. Faint voices, music, someone practicing playing a horn badly—the sounds of normal life. A hint of a breeze peeled back the heat. The warmth felt pleasant.

The dark figure which vaulted the fence separating Lucien's complex with the neighboring property moved quickly. It ran through the shadows on the opposite side of the street. An approaching vehicle stopped, and a door opened.

With his right eye, Miles zoomed in.

A limo. The passenger compartment lights were on, and he saw who was riding in back.

Svetlana Petroff.

And judging by the figure's height and general shape and what neighborhood they were in, she was picking up her star client and didn't want the militia troopers to see.

But Lucien wasn't getting in. Words were exchanged. From the passenger side came a large man who apprehended Lucien.

"Let go!"

The man was stronger and hauled Lucien into the back of the limo. The door slammed. The passenger compartment lights went out.

The limo made a five-point turn and headed back down the street. Miles started up the bike and followed.

Chapter Thirty-Four

They were heading into Bright Blocks.

Miles had seen enough of the neighborhood for a while, but could only guess they were returning to the scene of the crime. Surely the militia had the place sensored up. The silent alarm had caught him last time.

But what purpose could this trip serve? Red District and the sheriff had searched the location, no doubt multiple times. If the transponder had been hidden, it would have been found.

They didn't cross the berm to the junkyard. Instead, they cruised down the lane towards a large building.

Derelict vehicles stripped of doors, fenders, tires, and engines lined the street. Groups of huddled locals gathered around barrels of fire. Children ran about in the dancing gloom. Older youths pedaled about on bicycles. A vendor with a food cart with an open grill made skewers. The limo coasted past it all.

Miles shut off his lights and kept a hundred meters back, finally bringing the bike to a stop next to what had once been a driverless truck. The limo had parked in a sandy roundabout behind another car.

Miles took the key out and went on foot to get closer.

From the limo emerged two men Miles guessed were bodyguards. They had dark glasses despite the late hour, broad shoulders, and suits which might conceal a tactical jet fighter.

The skewer seller barked something at him in Mandarin, but Miles ignored her, pausing at the corner of a utility box covered in scrawl. Whoever normally ran this neighborhood was in hiding. But there were plenty of teens about, no doubt serving as their eyes and ears. The limo was being watched. Miles was, too. But whatever was going down was being allowed to happen. Or the neighborhood bosses were smart enough to know when they were outgunned.

Svetlana Petroff, Lucien Khar, and the gorilla who had apprehended him got out next. They met a waiting goon at the gate to the apartments, and they all vanished inside.

Miles followed.

The central courtyard was boxed in by the four-story complex on all sides. A concrete bunker-like structure dominated the center courtyard. Perhaps it had once been a community clubhouse. Now it looked like a redoubt in the center of a ruined city block.

The apartment building only had a dozen lights in the hundred windows looking out at the courtyard. Many of the balconies were missing, while some were little more than crumbling ledges. But residents were on many of these, legs dangling and watching silently as the procession moved towards the bunker. From somewhere, a baby wailed, and a woman was shouting angrily. Thrumming music blasted from a few of the apartments. The smell of fried foods, burned breadstuff, and garlic permeated the air.

Miles waited in the entryway until Svetlana and Lucien vanished. One guard was waiting outside and watched as Miles approached.

"Am I late?"

The man was reaching inside his jacket when Miles punched him in the center of his chest. The goon gasped. He would have collapsed, but Miles caught him and brought him along inside.

A weak light fixture buzzed above the main clubhouse room. The bare space was littered with rubbish and reeked of urine. A pair of older teens in sleeveless shirts stood on either side of a group of four young children. All girls, young, around ten, wearing simple clothes, shoulder length black hair, East Asian features.

Miles recognized a lineup when he saw one. Something else the girls all shared was a collection of cheap, colorful bracelets. Svetlana Petroff had one on her desk when Miles had visited her office.

The four terrified children kept their heads low, as if not wanting to make eye contact with the two men keeping them captive or any of the new arrivals. Everyone else stared at Miles.

He shoved the door guard down to the ground, but not before clearing a burner from the man's jacket. He tried gripping the weapon in his right hand, but with the broken finger it didn't feel right, so he switched.

"What are you doing here?" Svetlana blurted.

"I'm asking myself the same question. I'm here to see this thing finished."

The goon next to Lucien flexed his fingers. Both the guards by the girls appeared ready to bolt. But Svetlana set her jaw and closed in on Miles.

"Leave. This doesn't concern you."

"Let me tell you what I see here and correct me if I'm wrong. You've got four scared children who don't want to be here. You also snatched Lucien. The item that was up for grabs didn't just vanish. Someone took it. But while the militias and Meridian looked for me, for Lucien, or their own wayward agent, everyone but you missed the fact that there was someone else at the party. Maybe it was one of these girls. Am I on the right track?"

"This is your last chance to put that gun away and go."

"Lucien, have you tried firing your lawyer? Hostile customer service like this shouldn't be tolerated."

Svetlana's face turned a shade of beet red. "I love Lucien like a son. "

"Is that why that big ape had to pull him into your car? An upgrade over his other muscle, I see, and this one listens to you. Already getting used to how things will be now that you're in charge of Shahid Khar's empire."

"He's not left-handed, boss," the goon said. "And his right hand is busted. I can take him."

Miles shot him. The man dropped and howled, clutching a burn wound in his side. The guards by the girls stiffened and raised their hands. Lucien did too.

Svetlana barely flinched. "So you shoot with your off hand. Bravo."

"Come on, Lucien, let's get you home," Miles said.

Lucien hesitated. The cock-sure student presiding over his theater lackeys and the kid who had survived the torments of the Meridian interrogator were gone. He looked at Svetlana like a child who couldn't manage with his shoelaces.

Svetlana's face softened. "It's okay, Lucien. Your friend here doesn't understand this. And you don't have to tell him anything. I'll care for you. Once tonight is over, you won't have to do anything like this ever again."

"After tonight, you won't need him anymore, will you?" Miles asked.

"I don't know what you're talking about."

"You have Lucien tell you which of these kids was there the other night. They lead you to the transponder, don't really need him to run anything. Probably best if he's out of the way. You'll have enough money and clout to steal Shahid Khar's empire and make it your own."

"I would never hurt him."

"Maybe. But that didn't stop you from strong-arming him tonight."

"Lucien, tell Mr. Kim you're fine. Tell him to leave."

"I...I..." Lucien managed.

"Is that what you want, Lucien?" Miles asked. "Me to leave you here with her, with them?"

When Lucien remained silent, Svetlana laughed. "I'll take care of you, sweety. Never mind the nasty man. Now Mr. Kim, won't you put the gun away? You're scaring him and everyone else here, and you shot poor Mr. Brandt."

"Don't talk to me about scared," Miles said. "You've brought four girls here under duress and terrorized them."

"They haven't been harmed. Once we solve this, everyone gets a few credits to make the ouchies go away. That's the obvious solution, isn't it? A bump to whatever pittance Marshal Barma has paid you? You've proven capable. Perhaps a job offer? I'm sure your talents are worth the going rate."

"I'll pass. Lucien, it's time to decide."

The young man nodded. "I'd like to leave."

Svetlana rolled her eyes. "Well, you can't. At least not yet. This is ridiculous. We came this far. I need you to hold it together for a few more minutes. We find the item, and then you go back home. Which girl was it?"

Lucien looked at the children before pointing at the one on the far left. "Her, I think."

"Good. Now, Mr. Kim, you can watch as I have a friendly conversation with her so we can settle this matter. Not a hair on her head will be harmed." She crouched before the girl. "Hi, sweetie. I'm sorry these boys scared you. But I'm friendly. Why don't you tell me what happened the other night after you met that nice young man over there?"

"That's enough," Miles said. "Get away from her. Lucien—"

What happened next happened fast. Svetlana pivoted with the girl in her arms. She raised a small palm blaster that appeared out of nowhere and fired. The sharp *pop-pop-pop* echoed through the small chamber. Miles dove to the floor. Felt a sharp sting in his shoulder. The local toughs on either side of the girls were running. So were the other girls, one of them screaming at the top of her lungs. Lucien remained standing even as Svetlana was backing towards a rear exit, the girl in her arms. Her blaster moved about the room. The injured guard Miles had shot was crawling out of the way. The door guard had rolled to the cover of an alcove. From his ankle, he pulled a backup weapon.

"Get down!" Miles shouted at Lucien, but the young man remained frozen in place.

Miles sprang for him, knocking Lucien to the floor as more shots erupted from either side of them. White hot pain surged down his left side as he clutched Lucien with his metal arm. They landed hard on the ground, Miles shielding Lucien as puffs of smoke from the burner impacts exploded along the nearest wall. The searing agony made it hard to breathe. Miles rolled to his back, forcing his left hand to keep hold of the weapon, but the arm trembled as he felt himself growing weaker.

The door guard was on his feet. "I got him!" Grinning, he took a step forward, raising the burner.

"Take care of both of them," Svetlana ordered.

Miles felt a mountain weighing on his gun hand and it was only getting heavier. His burner tumbled from his grip, and he dropped his arm.

The guard had him and Lucien in his sights and the man's smile hardened. "Sorry, kid. The deal's too good. Nothing personal."

Chapter Thirty-Five

The bang and starburst which followed filled Miles' world with light and thunder, robbing him of all sense of direction, space, and time. Too numb for hell, too painful for heaven. But there was enough sensation from his mechanical arm to realize he still gripped Lucien even as pinpricks rolled up and down his skin. His face tingled. The splitting screeching in his ears was a sharp set of needles driving ever deeper. He couldn't blink away the afterimages of whatever had happened.

An explosion.

Didn't need Insight to know a burner wouldn't do that. Another flashbang. Meridian. Somehow they had found them.

And as much as his side and shoulder continued to throb from the burner rounds he had taken, he knew he was alive and the door guard hadn't fired.

He worked his jaw. Tried to sit up. A set of hands helped him. A muffled voice. Feminine. He was placed against a wall, steadied when he almost keeled over, and then left alone.

"Lucien?" he croaked.

But no one answered. He strained his left eye, willed his Insight module to start up again, but it was his artificial right eye which fed his brain the information he craved.

No one was in the clubhouse. No one standing, at least. The lamps had been destroyed in the explosion. Next to him lay sprawled the two guards. His poor night vision didn't give him enough detail to know if they were alive or not, but for the moment, neither moved.

Where was Lucien?

He lost track of what was hurting when he clenched his teeth and forced himself to stand. Concrete dust filled the air and choked his nostrils. An acrid chemical smell, perhaps residue from the grenade, stung his sinus and throat and coated his tongue. He absently touched his face and confirmed he was bleeding from his nose and lips. Contusions on his cheek and jaw.

Some kind of sting pellets in the flashbang, he guessed.

The type of party popper when you want people to survive. He checked both guards for a weapon. Nothing. He tottered across the room, scanning for any more bodies. Apparently, the children had gotten out, along with Svetlana. So had whoever chucked the grenade.

Locals?

Why would they bother to get him sitting up?

Only one other possibility.

He made it to the back entrance where a fire exit stood ajar, the automatic door closer dangling. Things were coming into view. The lights on the courtyard balconies were smears of light. Shapes moved in the darkness. Voices. Not English, at least not at first.

"Hey, mister, you don't look so good."

Miles tried to walk forward but decided it would be best to lean in the doorway for a little while until the world below him stopped spinning.

Dawn Moriti was staring at him. She was on her haunches and put a hand to his head and scraped crust from his eye.

"Can you walk?"

"On a good day, yes."

He leaned heavily as she guided him around the outside of the clubhouse towards the front of the apartment complex.

"What are you doing?" he asked.

"Saving you, at the moment. Since it looks like you weren't going anywhere, the locals might have decided you didn't need some of your parts. Lots of that going around."

"Lucien?"

"Took off. The lawyer slipped away too."

"Slipped away, or you shot them?"

She didn't answer.

When they made it to the entrance, he stopped to get a look at her. She wore a dark combat suit with no helmet. Bandages concealed half of her face. A compact submachine gun with a suppressor and reflex scope hung around one arm, along with a duffel bag.

"You have the transponder."

"Back to square one. Enough people know about it now that I don't know what I'm going to do yet. Get out of this neighborhood first, and figure it out from there."

"It's trouble. Meridian isn't going to stop. Neither will all the other interested parties."

"Maybe. But tell me, after your experience in the war, are you happy about how it all ended? You've been around long enough to see what's happened to us. Seraph, River City—is that enough for you?"

"I'm not a politician."

"You're human. We're heading full steam back to where we were hundreds of years ago. Look at this neighborhood, and it's barely a few decades old. Getting off this rock was humanity's one silver lining. This has a chance of getting us back out there."

"A lot of ifs. That thing needs to work. And if you're so altruistic, give it away. Give it to the university. Have them put the schematics on Seraph net, share it with New Pacific. Meridian won't be able to take it away."

Outside, the grill had closed shop. Dozens of people watched from the burning barrels. Everyone was keeping their distance. Even in the building foyer's darkness, Miles felt exposed.

"I'm going to put you on your motorcycle," Dawn said. "It's up to you what to do next. We're square now. But if you come after me, don't expect me to not shoot first."

She got him moving towards his bike. It was parked where he left it and appeared intact.

"How did you find the transponder?" he asked.

"Slipped you a tracing patch when you brought me home. It was still active when I came to, and once I got myself well enough to get up and pumped with more stims, I came searching."

"And the local kids?"

"My little angels. I was out of it when they found me. They did their best to patch me up. I'm guessing they took off when the scrappers came around. Then the scrappers brought the surgeon. Lucien must have run into one of the kids before the meet started. That's the bracelet thing I overheard them talking about, wasn't it?"

"Yeah. So it wasn't just one of them."

"Those girls found me and stabilized me before robbing me and taking the transponder. Probably thought it was worth a credit or two. Turns out no one wanted it. I'm not even mad. You have your bike key?"

He did. "You didn't hurt any of them?"

"Those kids are just trying to get by, like you and me. I traded for the transponder, and now their family has enough credits to give them a chance, if they can get out of this block."

"You're a veritable saint."

"And I don't need your approval. Worry about yourself on this one. You didn't make friends. You think Lucien Khar is going to be sending you Return Day messages? Sheriff going to forget you torpedoing her grab for power? You could come with me."

"What?"

"I'll get you fixed up. We can find others who don't want *this* to be our future."

"I fought my war. Seraph is my home now."

"Yeah. Figured you'd say that."

She got him leaning on his bike. So many questions. Who had first found the transponder? Did she really believe the Caretakers would sit idly by while someone built a spaceship to test their defenses? And what was her plan when the word spread that she had it?

"Destroy it," he finally said. But when he looked about, he discovered that Dawn Moriti had once again vanished.

Chapter Thirty-Six

When he tried to start the bike, the engine didn't turn. The palm-sized control panel wouldn't light up, either, and a quick examination revealed the low-voltage generator was missing, along with a few of the cables and the alternator.

He started pushing. It was a bad idea that only got worse when he realized the bike was a beast without power, plus he was hurt and exhausted.

He took a shortcut across a lot, passing several groups of locals dutifully avoiding eye contact. Had they been part of Svetlana Petroff's search for the girls who had found the transponder? Were they family who had been no doubt threatened by the thugs who had dragged the girls to the clubhouse? Or were they the thieves who had taken parts from his stolen motorcycle and were even now waiting to jump him to finish the job?

No, he decided. They were just enjoying the night as best they could and didn't want to get hassled any more than he did. Still, he didn't want to stop moving.

The tapping of metal pipes sounded from somewhere behind him. Same noise as what he had heard back in the junkyard after rescuing Dawn just before someone had thrown a bottle.

At a neighboring property, bright lights illuminated a basketball court. A sizeable group of people, young and old, were gathered. Someone played guitar while two women sang a bright, full-throated duet in Spanish. A man in a festive costume handed out whipped gelato from a dispenser.

Miles got closer.

Center court, a spider bot suspended on wires attached to an overhead boom was doing a whipsy-whirl dance of flips and pirouettes. It bounced high in a somersault to the delight of the collected audience.

Past the entertainment, a material printer was chugging away, putting the finishing touches on a large wok. A metal grinder whirred to life next to it as a woman in a greasy t-shirt threw lengths of scrap metal and plastics into the top of the machine. The clatter of rending steel drowned out the music for a few seconds before the operator killed the engine. She shoveled the resulting grist from a receptacle and loaded it into the printer.

A waiting man exclaimed his delight when the machine operator handed over the wok. She then went to work programming the printer, and it sprang to life on a new project. The next man had a bike missing some parts. The printer churned out a bike chain in no time flat.

One man's trash...

Miles stopped pushing. Couldn't go on, or didn't want to, he wasn't sure. But the motorcycle was heavy, his side ached, and his shoulder was in agony.

He went over to the woman operating the machines. "See that bike there? Can you use it for your recycler?"

It took her only a moment. "Wow. Yes, absolutely. Looks like she's in good shape, actually. Too good for the grinder, if you ask me."

"What is this, some kind of festival?"

"What, our neighborhood huddle? You new? This is what our neck of Bright Blocks does every night. 'Fight the dark with good,' right? Say, are you okay? You seem shaky."

"I'm okay." He handed her the key to the motorcycle. "Nothing I can't handle on my own."

He made it as far as the street, where he found a concrete base to a missing light pole to sit on. There he listened to the last song before the musicians quit. The crowd dispersed, and the recycler operator packed her machines into a cargo container. The lights went out. Somewhere in the distance, more pipes banged, with others answering, until it sounded like three separate percussionists rapping out messages.

Miles might have been resting for ten minutes or an hour. Wasn't sure when they showed up. It was at least five of them, with another five or maybe ten lurking further back in the shadows.

A lean man in a tank top squatted next to him and gave him a nudge. "You awake?"

"Let me guess. This is your turf."

The man shrugged. Smiled. Even in the faint light, Miles glimpsed gold among the man's front teeth. He also had a metal bat in his hand.

He nudged Miles with the bat. "You and your friends came onto our property and started some things."

"Not my friends."

"You almost got some of my family killed."

"Yeah. I have the name of the person who was in charge of what happened. A lawyer. Pretty good at what she does, if you got the money."

"You think you're funny. She's gone, and so are her soldiers. You got left behind."

"Not my crew. I followed them here to stop them from hurting anyone, including the girls they grabbed."

The gold teeth flashed in a sneer. "Two of them are my nieces."

"Your nieces got into something which got them in trouble. That trouble is gone now."

"You say that like you're happy about it."

"Yeah, I'm happy. It was bad news I've been chasing for the past two days, and it ended here. For your nieces' sake, it's good that it's over. For everyone's sake, maybe."

Gold Tooth poked Miles in the chest with the bat. "So we have you to thank?"

"I didn't start it, I didn't finish it. Maybe it won't be over, but I doubt anything will come back here to your neck of Seraph. The person responsible for breaking up that meeting is gone."

"This lawyer."

"No. Another lady who got herself messed up, and your nieces saved her. They then took something they couldn't have known would bring this kind of hassle to your front door."

Gold Tooth stood and consulted in hushed tones with two of the others before returning to Miles' side. "Sounds like maybe you did like you said and helped my family by sending those people away. My neighborhood looks out for its own. Don't need you or anyone else coming here dragging their fights into our block. Understand?"

Miles gave him a thumbs-up.

"So long as that's clear." Gold Tooth leaned closer. "But friend, you don't look so good."

"Just resting up. I'll be on my way in a bit."

Gold Tooth did some more consulting. Miles felt a fresh wave of dizziness when he tried to rise. Fell back. The shapes closed in on him.

If he knew where he'd wake up, he would have found the strength to laugh.

Chapter Thirty-Seven

The scalpel hovered near Miles' eye. Lights kept blinding him, the illumination radiating from two LEDs on either side of Dr. Brook's glasses.

"You shouldn't be awake. Nurse, he's awake."

A woman appeared over him, who Miles recognized from the Bright Blocks clinic. She had an anesthesia mask she brought up to Miles' face. Miles grabbed her by the wrist. She screamed, dropped the mask, tried to back away.

Dr. Brook tried to pry Miles' hand away. "Hey, dog! Let go! Let go! You're okay. No one's hurting you here."

Miles tried to move, but his body wasn't responding. Then he noticed he held the nurse with his cybernetic hand, and the missing finger had been replaced.

"You're all right," the doctor continued. "We're fixing you up, is all. You hurt her, and that's one more thing to add to your bill. Now hold still. I have work to do."

"Why can't I move?"

Dr. Brook smiled. "I sprung extra for local anesthetics. Can't have you wiggling around."

Miles let the nurse go. She retreated from the table. He examined his hand, turning and flexing it. The replaced finger was of a darker metal composite, and the joints looked different. The rest of his hand and right arm were polished and smelled of machine oil.

"Replacement digit is compatible," Insight volunteered. *"Driver update installed."*

"You got into my head," Miles said.

"Yeah. You want me to do this proper? Means I jack in. Hand, arm, eye firmware should all be updated now. That's some funky software you have in there, but that didn't stop me. Some local resources had what I needed ready to download for only a few credits. Whole module might be replaced with something a little more streamlined, but I don't know. There's something to be said about the old units like yours. But artificial skin would be the first thing if it were me, dog. You look like one of the metal heads with your rig. Plus, it draws attention."

"How much longer?"

"Not long. Putting another layer of skin regen on your burn. A rib took most of the damage, so I filled that. Lost some intercostal muscle tissue, which will be painful as it heals. You'll want follow-up appointments. Skin's going to be fine, but there's always the danger of infection. Lucky it didn't penetrate the chest cavity. Guessing we wouldn't be having this conversation if we did. Lung strike with a laser? Yeesh."

"What about my shoulder?"

"Superficial. Skin and muscle. May I suggest armor the next time you get into a burner fight?"

"Just...finish up."

The doctor crouched over him for a moment, applying something which hissed with a sharp jet of compressed air. Then he looked up again at Miles. "I recognize your implants. Thought they looked familiar once I got into the make and model. Dog, did we have an appointment a few weeks ago?"

Miles winced when he took in a breath too fast. "Don't tell me. That was you?"

"Things sometimes come full circle. After you get my bill, you may need to reconsider what you do with your particular assets. Speaking of assets, what did you do with my motorcycle, dog?"

***

It didn't feel like sleep.

The pleasant numbness which had washed over him had snuck up and knocked him out without him realizing it. The next thing Miles knew, he was in a hospital room, the aches and pains gone, and the world smothered by a soft pillow.

Insight scrolled hundreds of pages past his field of vision. He could have ignored it, sinking back down into the bliss of unconsciousness. But then he reminded himself where he lay and who the doctor was. And as he recalled the events of the previous night, he knew he couldn't go back to sleep.

Images flashed in the corner of his eye. What was Insight doing? He blinked hard to pull up the interface.

Everything was different. Clunky tabs were replaced with colored overlays. With a thought, Insight showed him traffic, a newsfeed, a sale promotion at a grocery store, job listings, a weather report.

"Insight? What is this?"

"Seraph net. The enhanced uplink node has a wider range, with automatic updates—"

"We're online?"

"Yes. In anticipation of setup preferences, I've begun cataloging a backlist of items on the net which might interest you—"

"Shut up. Hold on. Turn off uplink."

"Uplink ended."

"And turn off every automatic process. Check with me first, understood?"

"Understood."

Miles' heart hammered in his chest. He took a moment to calm down before climbing out of bed. Had the doctor adjusted the Insight settings? The last thing he wanted was for his brain module to be online while he was asleep. With people like the Meridian agents out there, it was like shining a spotlight into the sky.

He needed a phone. Needed a burner. Needed to get out of there.

He paused before dismissing Insight's screen. Expanded it so it filled his vision. While Seraph net was only a city-wide service, it received unofficial information dumps from sources in both River City and New Pacific. He scanned the headlines.

Yellow Tigers Parent Company Elects New CEO.

Xander Trowbridge Found Dead in Bright Blocks. Suspected Suicide.

Downtown Bombing Investigation Yields Links to Anarchists. Town Meeting Scheduled to Address Terrorist Threat.

Scrolling further, he finally found anything which mentioned Bing Patton.

Yellow Tiger Chief Passes Away After Fight with Cancer.

No mention of Shahid Khar, Lucien, Meridian, or any showdown between the militias. As an afterthought, he searched for himself or anything the marshals had done, but he found nothing. A silver lining to the less-than-robust news services of his newly adopted city.

With a hard blink, he cleared Insight away and went to find his clothing.

Miles had guessed it was morning, but the sun was in the southwest. For everything Insight could now do, the time hadn't been set, and he had been out for longer than expected. Heat waves rolled off the tops of the nearest crate stacks. The air tasted thick. The few residents who were outside the Bright Blocks clinic appeared to be trying to move as little as possible and stuck to the shade.

Tristan rolled up out front in his three-wheel tuk-tuk. He leaned forward on the steering wheel. "Lost your phone again?"

"When the nurse said she'd call you, I didn't know if you'd come."

He spread his arms as if to say, "Ta-da! I'm here."

"Take me home."

After a few minutes of navigating his way through the Bright Block streets, Tristan glanced at Miles sheepishly. "Manager fired you."

"Figured as much."

"I can tell him you got attacked. That you're sick. That you'll be back."

"Not sure if I'm coming back."

"You gotta eat. You gotta pay rent. I can spare you a few credits, but things are tight with the kids."

"A ride to the hotel is what I need."

"I can quit too. Maybe then he'll have to take both of us back. We could be like a union or something. Collective bargaining. Right?"

Miles hung on as they rounded a corner. A wave of nausea took a moment to pass. "Don't do that. You don't have to feel guilty that you still have a job. I made my choices; here I am. I'll be fine."

"You don't look fine," Tristan said in a small voice. "Just saying."

Tristan brought him back to his hotel on Gallina Road. "I'll help you to your room."

"I'll make it. Thanks. I appreciate it more than you can imagine."

Someone who wasn't the manager was mopping the lobby. The air smelled...clean.

The teen wore a collared shirt and khakis. "Resident?"

"Yeah," Miles said. "Paid up for the week."

"Your ID?"

He presented the card key and hoped it would do. "Where's the manager?"

"You're looking at him. Old Cash had a heart attack last night. I'm his son Wyatt. No drugs. No guests. No hookers. No noise after 9pm. Tomorrow the door gal comes, and you'll need your key to get into the lobby. You have a problem with that?"

"Nope. No problem at all."

Some things resolved themselves.

After washing up, he took stock. The Bright Blocks gang had relieved him of his remaining credits. He hadn't decided if they had taken him to Dr. Brook with the idea of selling his parts or if they had wanted to save him.

Didn't matter, he reckoned.

His stomach grumbled. He figured he could start walking and make the charity kitchen dinner service if he set out immediately. After that, find a phone and make sure Dillan and Zoe were okay. He had a dog to retrieve. Probably a dozen other loose ends, but judging by the headlines, Seraph was moving on.

He had saved Lucien Khar, hadn't he? Assuming Dawn hadn't killed him. Somehow he believed her that Lucien still lived.

The son of the information broker would have to navigate his own life from now on, and if he decided to let Svetlana Petroff to take over, it was on him. With the transponder gone and once again in Dawn Moriti's hands, the situation could just as easily start up again. But for now, he could sit it out. It would take a week of sleep before he could digest everything. Probably had a warrant out for his arrest. Surely, the sheriff and the militias knew where to find him. But they could wait until after dinner.

***

The new manager was in the lobby and spoke with a raised voice. "I can't share that information with you. We have a strict no visitor policy."

Dillan stood facing him. "If you won't let me past, at least call up to the room."

"I'm not a messaging service. There's no phone in the room you're asking about. And I won't tell you whether anyone's home or not."

His son held his ground. "It's my father up there. He may not be well."

Miles stepped down the last of the stairs. "Dillan?"

Wyatt had stopped his son in the doorway. Dillan craned his neck and the manager let him pass. Dillan came forward, only to pause. "Dad, what happened to you? I've been trying to call. Then I got a message telling me first you were in a clinic in Bright Blocks and then you were back here."

"A message from who?"

"It was anonymous. Thought maybe it's your cop friend with a private number."

Or Dawn was still tracking him with a bug. Time to replace all his clothes and scrub down.

"I'm fine. There was more trouble. I lost my device."

Dillan looked Miles over. "Let's go get you one, then. Can you tell me what happened?"

"It's a long story. I don't know if you want to hear it."

They left the hotel. Dillan's silver car was across the street.

"I'm still mad at you, dad. You could have gotten Zoe hurt, or worse. If something happened to her—"

"Nothing did."

"Will you let me finish? If anything had happened, I could never forgive you. Roping her into your investigation put her life on the line. You understand that, right?"

"Yes."

Dillan nodded. His nostrils flared. He fumbled with the key as he tried to get the car started. He got it going on the third attempt. They drove to the nearby drugstore. Dillan parked and set the brakes before taking a deep breath and facing his father.

"Some of the things in the news...you were involved. I don't think I want to know. It's your business if you decide to become a cop again. But this isn't River City. The news only tells a little of what happens around Seraph. There's a lot of bad people here. Some good ones, too, but things are different."

"I'm getting the sense of that."

"What I mean is...I don't know what I'm trying to say. Telling you to be careful? Won't happen. You're you. But I love Zoe."

"I screwed up. I won't involve either of you in my work. I promise."

Dillan had broken off eye contact again. Was nodding too eagerly. "Let's get you your phone."

Chapter Thirty-Eight

The crew of students on the university theater stage erected the last piece of scenery, a fabricated backdrop of a parlor wall painted in white and pink, with a false window and door, along with a mantle holding a vase with drooping flowers.

Lucien Khar stood at the corner of the stage. He wore a black mock turtleneck sweater and tight slacks. "Tilt it more. It's meant to be off center. There. That's right."

Miles had entered the auditorium through an open side door. When Lucien saw him, he dropped off the stage and met him halfway down the center aisle. No one was close enough to overhear.

"You survived," Lucien said.

"Yeah. So did you."

"This isn't a proper rehearsal. You should wait until next Thursday for a preview. I'll make sure you get tickets."

"I'm not here for that. I'm looking in on you. Wasn't sure if you made it."

Lucien spread his arms. "Here we both are. Is there some business we didn't finish? Are you hoping for a thank you? A returned favor? Payment?"

"No. I was doing my job."

"Then why are you interrupting me?"

Miles tried to ease the tension in his voice. "When we spoke at your home, you made a point to tell me you learned where my son works. In case it was more than you flexing how much you know, I'm here as a reminder that I'm the one you'll need to deal with if we have a problem. Not my son. Not anyone else. Us."

Now that they were standing close, it was obvious Lucien was wearing a heavy layer of makeup. It didn't quite cover the swelling, bruises, and cuts marking his face. One student had approached with a tablet in hand, but she hung back.

Miles made a quick survey of the rest of the theater. "Your bodyguards are gone."

"I don't want them here."

"Your father's business?"

"Svetlana can have it," Lucien said firmly. "I quit."

"You trust her enough to do that after what she pulled?"

"No. But what choice do I have? I told her what I want. She said she'd respect my decision."

"And she'll support you while she runs the intelligence operation."

"That's...none of your business."

"You're right. It's not."

Miles left the theater. If Svetlana Petroff was going to honor her arrangement with Lucien after everything, then perhaps Miles had misread her. She had wanted them both dead back at Bright Blocks. Perhaps that had changed. With the transponder off the table, she might need Lucien after all.

But Miles was a loose end. Would she come after him?

Not for the moment. Besides being a witness to her actions, he had nothing on her. And he had his own legal trouble. Their paths had no reason to cross. And he guessed if Lucien was content in his life as a thespian, she would be free to operate Shahid Khar's network as she pleased.

***

With a ringing chord and plenty of reverb, Dillan's band played.

Miles had heard enough of it from his previous nights out to understand it wasn't just a wall of noise. The dissonance coalesced and occasionally came through with a pleasing refrain before setting off on a fresh course of unfamiliar sounds, never letting the listener settle on a theme or find a melody. And just as suddenly, the tune ended.

The next number stood in stark contrast: gentle, repeating, building to something, and delivering an emotional, melancholic refrain which was familiar. Miles realized he had heard it before and, even more surprising, realized he liked the piece.

At the other tables, heads bobbed to the rhythm. Smiles. Most of the conversations had died as something of a spell settled over the crowd. Miles turned the teacup around on its base and considered the vacant chair opposite him.

She wasn't coming.

Fair enough.

They went out when Miles had invited her the first time he had gone to see Dillan play and two times after. She had told him not to have any expectations. They were never dates.

When the dog rushed up and jammed its muzzle into his lap, he almost jumped from his chair. Santabutra Sin sat down across from him and waved a server over.

"The white ale, please."

The server hurried off as she settled in. The dog wedged itself near Miles' feet.

He ran his hands on the dog's head. Caught a whiff of soap. "I'm pretty sure there're no pets allowed in here. Did you give him a bath?"

"He was filthy. And I checked at the door. They don't have a problem with well-behaved animals."

"I didn't think you'd come."

"Ghosting's not my style. If I was going to break plans with you, I would have called. They played this one last time, didn't they?"

"Yeah. I think the song's growing on me."

The beer arrived. She sipped it. Nodded her approval. Drank some more.

The band moved on to a third number, a syncopating rhythm-heavy mood piece with shifting violet and blue lights cast about the stage. The performers looked like shadows. Dillan started in on a guitar adagio, which mesmerized.

Both Miles and Santabutra tried to speak at the same time.

"Go ahead," she conceded.

"I'm sorry you got in trouble for what I did."

She waved it off.

Miles rotated the teacup again. "I'm serious. Like you said, you put your job at stake. Your pension. And we barely know each other."

"It was the right thing to do. I made my choice because I know the kind of man you are. What I can't fathom is why you put so much on the line for a piece of trash like Lucien Khar."

"He's slime. But he didn't deserve to lose his life just because I don't like him."

"He wasn't the job."

"He wasn't. Barma wanted me to find out what happened in the junkyard. Lucien was there because his father needed a driver. Then he was abducted by the Meridian agents and kidnapped again by his lawyer."

"Yellow Tigers are still sorting that out. No one's talking. It's twice that you risked everything to find him. You also stepped up with your friend Dawn. I'm thinking they'd both be dead if not for you. A lesser person would have let it go. You served. You did your part. You have a son who you're getting to know, and you earned it. Yet you put your neck on the line for strangers."

"And if I was that person who let it go, would you be here with me tonight?"

She drank her beer and watched the stage. The lights shifted to deep reds and yellows. The music had quickened, the soft piece now rising with a heavy synth bass. Dillan was in the zone as sweat reflected on his brow. When the piece abruptly ended, the band bowed. The audience erupted in applause. Santabutra put fingers to her lips and whistled. She wasn't going to answer the question.

The dog shifted at his feet.

"Was this rascal any trouble?" Miles asked.

"We're talking about the kids now? Usually it's the sign the marriage is on its last legs if that's the best we can do."

"Fair enough," Miles said. "How is it going with your review? Any word of how the restructuring is going to change your organization."

"Relax, Kim. I'm pulling your leg. And I don't want to talk about work. You're here, be here. Enjoy the music. You mind if I order another beer?"

A brown ale replaced the empty glass. Miles had some tea as the band started in on a bouncy tune with an animated laser effect gyrating above them.

"I washed him," Santabutra said. "Local shop had a flea shampoo I used. I kept the receipt. You ever wonder why the dog took to you?"

"No clue. He showed up at the construction site. Never been good with animals. He's a naughty dog."

"The good ones are. But he's not real."

"What?"

She smirked. "I thought you were a detective. I didn't notice until I brought him home and washed him in the garage. He's artificial. High end. Nothing on the records of any model like this having been stolen. No one posted about it being missing. Strange, if you ask me, because he's probably worth as much as a new car, if not more. There are a few outfits who sell these things, if you feel like checking."

"Well, I guess that solves whether I can keep him in my room. But he ate and drank."

"Artificial animals will do that. But you have to occasionally clean out their insides if they do. Better download a user manual to know how."

A fake. Miles laughed. The dog had fooled him, and why not? He hadn't even imagined such a thing would be running around loose on the streets of Seraph. But who lost it would be a mystery for tomorrow. He put his hand down and petted the dog, felt its warmth, heard it whine when the horn player screeched a high note. Wondered if the dog smell was a feature.

"You're real enough for me," he said to the dog.

Santabutra glanced at him. "What?"

"Nothing. Just talking to my friend."

Miles and Santabutra tried to end the evening with a hurried goodbye, but Dillan met them out back before they could leave. The band had a waiting group of friends who appeared to be in a hurry to go somewhere to celebrate.

Santabutra gave Dillan a hug. "Great set. Amazing as always."

Dillan appeared nervous and uncomfortable. "Thanks. A bit choppy. I missed a couple of cues, almost threw everyone off."

"No one noticed, I'm sure."

"Where's Zoe?" Miles asked.

"She stayed in," Dillan said. "Needed some downtime."

"Tell her we say hi. Go be with your friends. I'll text you tomorrow. And Dillan? I'm proud of you."

Miles watched as Dillan and his group departed. A string trio was getting ready to enter the club. They were dressed as marionettes with stark white makeup and bright red lipstick, along with hats with bells.

"That's my cue to leave," Santabutra said.

"Yeah."

They squeezed through the crowd milling about out front and made it across the street where Miles had parked his latest bike. It was almost as large as Dr. Brook's big wheel monstrosity and longer than most sedans. Crimson red fenders, brushed steel pipes, a little rust on the chassis, and it leaked transmission fluid.

"Where'd you find that?" she asked.

"Barma offered me a permanent job. Then someone listed the bike for sale this morning. I needed a ride."

She smirked. "You barely survived the last time you worked with him. What did you tell him?"

"He came through with a paycheck this morning."

"And what made you spend your precious credits on this eyesore?"

"Gets me from point A to point B."

"For all your modesty, you're a showoff."

"No, I'm not."

"Your arm and shiny head and bright eye. You're not ashamed of what you are, and that's good. But after this week, I understand you have people out for you. There's such a thing as keeping a low profile. And now this bike?"

"I can't keep calling other people to get around. Thanks for coming out again."

"My pleasure."

"Dillan plays next Friday. A place called The Old Smoking Club."

"Never heard of it. Sounds dreary. But I'd love to be there. So are we doing this?"

Miles tightened his mouth. "Doing what?"

"This. Us. If we are, then we don't have to limit it to seeing your son play, as much as I enjoy it."

"I don't know. Are we? You said you weren't interested in dating."

"Dating is an activity which is exhausting on every level. But being social with people I care about is good for me, as much as I want to veg out at home with a book. So which is it, detective?"

"Did I tell you I'm not good at this? Rusty doesn't cover it. Yes, I want to see you. I don't know Seraph or any places to go. A cheap outing is the best I can manage right now. Free is even better. And I wasn't an actual detective."

"Detective. Cop. Same ballpark. We trip over clues and catch bad guys and hope, at the end of the day, we did more right than wrong. I work for a for-profit paramilitary organization responsible for policing the best hope for civilization free from corporate tyrants. My boss got killed trying to acquire a piece of tech which would have placed him and two criminal overlords at the top of a new food chain which would oppress the people I'm sworn to protect. It would have been as bad, if not worse, than anything Meridian managed during its years of dominance. I know I did right in what went down and I believe you did, too. Tomorrow, who knows?"

"Then let's check in with each other tomorrow and see where it leads."

He watched her drive off. The dog bumped his leg and looked up at him with eyes which caught the glow of the streetlights. Then, without prompting, it jumped to the seat of his motorcycle.

"All right, dog. Time to get you home."

I hope you enjoyed reading *A Haunt of Jackals*.

If you have a moment, please leave a rating or review.

Even a short comment can help independent authors find new readers. I also appreciate hearing feedback from my readers. You can get in touch through my social media links at IOAdler.com.

Miles Kim has a new case! *The Gallows of Heaven* is coming out in Spring, 2022.

Miles Kim's first day as Seraph's newest marshal may be his last.

When an escaped fugitive leads Miles on a chase into the remote southern barrens, he discovers a dead body lying next to a secluded spring.

But solving the murder and keeping his fugitive alive becomes complicated when a communication blackout prevents him from calling for backup.

Cut off, Miles finds himself in the sights of an enigmatic judge serving his own brand of outlaw justice.

Run or fight, Miles will need every trick in his arsenal to avoid becoming the next marshal to disappear in the savage wastelands.

Keep reading for an excerpt.

The Gallows of Heaven

Late morning, and they were speeding across a stretch of hardpan. The sun was bright on the dirty windshield and Miles had a hard time seeing through a cloud of dust.

A six-wheel buggy raced before them. Miles zoomed in. The corner of one fender bore the Yellow Tiger logo. The buggy weaved around the rocks and clusters of acacia. They were climbing in elevation, approaching a high hill with sheer cliffs. The dog leaned forward, ears up, and intent on the vehicle they were pursuing. The buggy took a track barely wide enough for its fat tires.

Marshal Jodie didn't hesitate to follow, leaning on the horn. "Pull that rig over!" he shouted over the runner's loudspeaker. But the buggy didn't slow even as it crested the ridge path and bounded over a line of jagged rocks. When the runner struck the obstacle, the sharp jolt of the vehicle's bottom hitting unyielding stone felt like the car was going to crack wide open.

Barma's voice crackled over the radio. "You have him?" *Crackle.* "...have him. Can't..." *Crackle-crackle.* "Reading me?"

"Do not copy, chief," Jodie said. "Repeat, do not copy. But we're in pursuit."

"Suspect is..." The rest of Barma's call vanished in the static.

Miles checked his burner before sliding it back into his shoulder holster. They followed the buggy up a winding trail along the top of the ridge. They were heading for a series of broken rocks which neither vehicle could cross unless they sprouted wings.

Jodie grinned. "Gotcha!"

It was impossible to see the buggy in the rising wave of chalky dust. Then their runner hit something. The collision caused the vehicle to lurch upward and spin out before landing back down on its tires. Red lights blinked from the dash. Jodie kept gunning the engine but the engine had quit.

"Stay," Miles ordered the dog.

He unclipped the seatbelt harness and climbed out, dropping for cover and waiting for the bank of dust to settle. Jodie let out a slew of curses as he fumbled with his own restraints before unceremoniously tumbling out of the car, which teetered atop a lump of rock beneath the chassis.

Jodie took a moment to get his balance before straightening his hat. "Hey, jackass!" he shouted at the Yellow Tiger buggy. "Get over here now!"

"Get down," Miles hissed.

"Nonsense. Whoever's driving that thing knows when they're licked."

Jodie marched forward. Miles hesitated for a second before joining him, his eyes scanning the haze for any signs of movement.

The buggy had its rearmost tires off the ground. It had collided straight on into a set of boulders. The driver's side gull door stood open. Deployed airbags lay deflated on the driver's seat. No driver, and no one hiding behind the vehicle.

"Seriously?" Jodie said. "It's too hot for this. Too hot! Hey, jackass—"

Miles grabbed his arm. "Keep your head down. He might be armed."

"Yeah, maybe. But if they start shooting, we get to shoot back. Barma said you're loaded to the gills with combat mods."

"I don't have combat modifications. Insight can target lock, but with all this dust, our burners are useless."

"That's your first mistake. Burners are toys for pimps and a show for spit and polish militia brats. You want people out here to respect you, bring a real gun."

As if to underscore the comment, Jodie cleared a long-barrel pistol from a thigh holster. Past the buggy was a gap in the boulders. Jodie took the lead, squeezing through to an uneven path which climbed ever upward.

Miles looked for a way where they could split up, but found none. With rocks above and all around them, even a lone defender could ambush them both with little effort. He kept his weapon raised and eyes moving.

"You stole that car. We caught you fair and square," Jodie shouted. "Looks like you're hung up. You don't want us to abandon you all the way up here, do you?" When no answer came, Jodie chambered a round in his weapon. "Hard way it is."

A spatter of blood on the rock. Miles pointed to it but Jodie kept walking.

Miles stopped him. Whispered, "Hold up. He's hurt."

"That'll make this easier."

"Why would someone steal a Yellow Tiger vehicle?"

"I've stopped trying to understand the criminal mind. Are we done? It's hot out and I want to catch this guy."

"He's down a vehicle, on foot, and injured. He won't get far. Let me try."

Jodie motioned for Miles to walk ahead of him. "Suit yourself."

"Cover me."

Miles inched forward to where the rock passage opened wide. A graveled slope ran down to a shaded gulley with a black pool of water. Plenty of boulders to hide behind. A formation of crumbling rock stood above it. At the crest, gnarled trees with a smattering of anemic yellow leaves rose from the tortured ground as if skeletal fingers reaching into the sky.

"This is Deputy Marshal Kim. I know you're hurt. I want to help you get out of here alive."

He slid down a section of loose shale. Scanned the ground. Another few blood drops near a jagged outcropping. He let out a sharp exhale before getting closer. Miles was exposed. If the perp was armed, he'd have a perfect shot.

"My gun's put away. We're not Yellow Tiger. We're with the marshals, and this is your best opportunity to walk out of this in one piece. I can get you medical help."

Feet were visible on the ground. Miles edged closer. The car thief was lying on his side and wearing soft footwear, like slippers, and lime green pants. A pale young man with a sunburned face. He had his arm curled against his chest and wrapped in a blood-soaked rag. The green pants were part of a jumpsuit all the same color. He raised his good hand to shield the sunlight from his eyes. Blinked and smiled.

"Good Sir Marshal, we meet again."

You may also enjoy these science fiction and fantasy novels published by Lucas Ross Publishing

The Minders' War series by Gerhard Gehrke

For Deanne and her correctional facility work crew, the night the stars fell ended everything.

Refuge

The Glass Heretic

The Children of Magus

The Goblin Reign series by Gerhard Gehrke

They razed Spicy's village, kidnapped his sister, and never imagined what one lone goblin would do to get her back!

Goblin

Goblin Apprentice

Goblin Rogue

Goblin War Chief

Goblin Outcast

The Old Chrome series by I.O. Adler

The Seraph Engine

The Atomic Ballerina
A Haunt of Jackals
The Gallows of Heaven

Fallen Rogues

A city of rogues. A seedy bar. A thief who stole the wrong prize.
The Midnight Monster Club
The Dragon and Rose
The Chapel of the Wyrm
The Isle of the Fallen

Milton Keynes UK
Ingram Content Group UK Ltd.
UKHW020134220823
427215UK00015B/904